PRAISE FOR
Just Like Me

"From pillow fights to pinkie promises, sock wars to s'mores, a red thread connects this energetic summer camp story with Julia's deeper journey to accept herself, her adoption, and her Chinese roots."

—Megan McDonald, award-winning and bestselling author of the Judy Moody series and Sisters Club trilogy

"A tender and honest story about a girl trying to find her place in the world and the thread that connects us all."

—Liesl Shurtliff, author of
Rump: The True Story of Rumpelstiltskin

"A heartwarming story about the universal struggle of yearning to be an individual while longing to fit in."

—Karen Harrington, author of *Sure Signs of Crazy*

"[A] charming and refreshingly wholesome coming-of-age story... Filled with slapstick humor and fast-paced action."

—*School Library Journal*

"Incredibly moving."

—*Kirkus Reviews*

Also by Nancy J. Cavanaugh

This Journal Belongs to Ratchet

Always, Abigail

Just Like Me

Elsie Mae Has Something to Say

Nancy J. Cavanaugh

sourcebooks
jabberwocky

Published by Sourcebooks Jabberwocky, an imprint of Sourcebooks, Inc.
P.O. Box 4410, Naperville, Illinois 60567-4410
(630) 961-3900
Fax: (630) 961-2168
www.sourcebooks.com

Library of Congress Cataloging-in-Publication data is on file with the publisher.

Source of Production: Versa Press, East Peoria, Illinois, USA
Date of Production: July 2017
Run Number: 5009903

Printed and bound in the United States of America.
VP 10 9 8 7 6 5 4 3 2 1

For Ron, because an adventure is always better when you have it with your best friend.

The summer I got Huck was my best summer and my worst summer, all wrapped into one.

It all started with the letter I wrote to President Roosevelt.

Chapter 1

Elsie Mae," Mama scolded, "where've ya been? Uncle Owen's been waiting on ya almost an hour now."

Mama stood in the yard with her hands on her hips, watching me hurry up toward the house. Uncle Owen sat on the porch swing with a jar full of tea.

"Sorry, Mama," I said. "I had somethin' I had t'do."

"Sounds mighty important," Uncle Owen said, licking his lips and grinning.

I gave him a quick peck on the cheek.

"I'll jus' be a minute," I said over my shoulder as the screen door clapped behind me.

I knew Uncle Owen didn't mind waiting on me. He always said he was the slow-moving, savoring sort.

"Sounds like a girl who don't mind her elders," I heard

Mama say as I headed down the hallway toward the back of the house.

She held a clothespin between her teeth, so she sounded even madder than I knew she was.

I heard Uncle Owen's voice again, and though I couldn't make out what he was saying, I knew he was probably defending me. Even so, I knew Mama wasn't paying any mind to whatever he said because before I made it to the bedroom, she hollered through the yard, past the screen door, and down the hall, "I tol' ya to be ready right after yer chores, didn't I?"

She must have clipped that clothespin back on the line by now because she couldn't have yelled *that* loud if it was still in her mouth.

Mama was the opposite of Uncle Owen. She was the fast-moving, getting-things-done sort. She probably got more done before breakfast than most folks got done all day. That wasn't the problem though. The problem was her expecting all of us kids to be the getting-things-done sort too.

With Mama, no school in the summer just meant she thought up more stuff for us to do. And Daddy was just as bad. He owned the store in town, and he expected all three of my older brothers to waste their entire summer separating nuts and bolts into different bins, dusting the shelves, and carrying packages for customers.

The only worse way to waste the summer was in our house with my three older sisters arguing over whose turn it was to do which chore, and then having Mama remind us all day long that we'd never find husbands if we kept on being so ornery.

Husbands! Who said anything about wanting a husband? My heart was set on getting a dog. Dogs were the best companions in the world. Grandpa Zeke had told me so.

He said, "Can't always trus' a man, but ya can pretty darn near always trus' yer dog."

As soon as I was old enough to be on my own, I planned to have a whole slew of dogs.

Once I got to the crowded bedroom I shared with my three sisters, I grabbed the flour sack I used to carry my things. It had been packed since last week.

Somehow, the gods of summer had shined down on me because for the last five years, I had spent the entire summer at Grandma Sarah's and Grandpa Zeke's house. It was the absolute best place to be in the summer—or any time of year, for that matter. They lived on Honey Island in the Okefenokee Swamp.

The whole arrangement had started the summer Mama broke her leg. She had fallen off the kitchen table while she was stretching to get a cobweb off the ceiling. I was only six that year, but Mama's broken leg turned out to be the best thing that ever happened to me. Since I was the youngest in our family and, according to Mama, the busy-getting-into-trouble sort, Mama decided to send me to Grandma and Grandpa's for the summer.

I may not have been the smartest in our family, but I was smart enough to figure out real quick that being the *only* kid at Grandma and Grandpa's house was about a thousand times better than being the youngest kid at my own house.

My brothers and sisters thought I was crazy.

"What do ya do all day?" my brothers asked.

And, "Aren't ya 'fraid the gators 'ill eat ya up?" my sisters wanted to know.

But even though the gators truly were one of the only things I was afraid of in the Okefenokee, I would just shrug and try not to smile too much because I didn't want them to ever find out how much they were missing. I liked things the way they were—me in the swamp and my brothers and sisters in town. After all, I wouldn't want any gators to get them.

So, every year, right after school let out, Uncle Owen

showed up to take me to Honey Island. And usually on the day he came to pick me up, I was ready and waiting. But today was different. Today mailing that letter had been really important.

I reached into the pocket of my overalls and took out a copy of the letter I had just mailed. I unfolded it and smoothed it out.

"Elsie Mae!" Mama hollered. "What in tarnation is takin' ya so long in there?"

"Comin'!" I yelled, stuffing the piece of paper back into my pocket without even folding it.

I headed down the hall with my flour-sack bag in my hand and hope in my heart. Hope that my letter might just make the difference I wanted it to.

Chapter 2

After I said my good-byes, Uncle Owen and I jumped into the wagon he'd borrowed from Josiah and headed down the dirt road. Josiah's old ox pulled us along toward Cowhouse Landing, the place where Uncle Owen always left his boat when he came up to our place for a visit.

Josiah was an old friend of Grandpa's. He lived in a clapboard shack a ways back from the edge of the swamp. He used his porch as a store and sold things to folks who lived in the Okefenokee. That way the swampers didn't have to come all the way in to town to buy coffee and flour and salt to bring back to their kitchens.

When Uncle Owen came to visit us, he always stayed with Josiah since there wasn't an inch of extra space in our crowded house for even one more person.

"Hard to believe I been comin' to pick ya up every summer since you was a li'l bitty thing," Uncle Owen said as we bounced along toward Josiah's.

I looked over at him. Grandma called us two peas in a pod, which was fine by me. Saying I was like Uncle Owen was like saying I was the smartest, nicest person in all of Charlton County.

"And look at ya now, practically all growed up," he said. "Sometime soon ya probly won't want to have anythin' t'do with yer ol' Uncle Owen cuz you'll have the boys followin' ya 'round." He elbowed me in the side.

"Boys?" I exclaimed. "Not me! Ya know I'm aimin' to git myself a dog as soon as I can."

"Oh, that's right," Uncle Owen said, smiling. "I do r'member ya mentionin' a time or two 'bout wantin' yer own dog."

I elbowed him right back. I knew he was teasing me. I hadn't just *mentioned* wanting a dog. I talked about it all the time.

"Yeah, but ya know Mama and Daddy'll never agree to it," I said. "So I'll probly have to wait till I actually am all growed up."

As we got farther and farther from home, the trees got

thicker and thicker. And as the road got smaller and smaller, the branches brushed up against us as Josiah's ox, Selly, pulled us along. I thought about telling Uncle Owen about the letter I'd just mailed, but the thing was, I didn't want to get his hopes up. I wasn't really sure if the letter would work. And even if it did, I kind of wanted it to be a surprise.

A week earlier, I had made the mistake of telling Mama about the letter. I was helping her with supper, and for some reason, my sisters weren't around with all their usual squawking.

It was the perfect time to tell Mama about my plan, but when I told her what I aimed to do, the first thing she had said was, "Now, Elsie Mae, why in tarnation would ya send a letter to the White House?"

And when I explained the whole story, instead of being proud of me for wanting to do something really important, she had said, "Elsie Mae, what makes ya think the president is goin' to listen to some eleven-year-old girl?" Then she said what she always says. "Instead of worryin' 'bout savin' the world, why don't ya worry more 'bout savin' yerself from gittin' in trouble by mindin' yer elders?"

With all her getting-things-done ways, Mama just couldn't see how minding my elders and doing my chores on time could *never* be the same as doing something big and important in the world.

With three older brothers and three older sisters, someone other than me was *always* getting noticed for doing something good. Davis with his best-in-the-class grades always made Mama and Daddy smile. Catherine was already a perfect seamstress, and Mama wasn't shy about bragging on her to the ladies in the Women's Missionary Society at church. Jack was on his way to becoming Daddy's best clerk at the store, and that made Daddy about as proud as a peacock. And the list went on and on. The problem was that I never even made the list.

But the thing was, I didn't want to get noticed for good grades or straight stitches or selling things in Daddy's store. I wanted to do something bigger than that. Something better. Something that would make people say, "Now that Elsie Mae is really *somethin'*!"

But I didn't want them to say I was really something because I dropped Mama's three-layer coconut cake on the way to the church fund-raiser or because I split open a fifty-pound bag of flour in Daddy's store the day I was in such a big hurry to go fishing. I wanted Mama and Daddy and everyone to say, "That Elsie Mae is somethin' awful darn special," but mean it in a good way. I was keeping my fingers crossed that the letter I had just mailed to the president of the United States was finally my chance to do that.

After traveling for an hour or so, Uncle Owen and I came around the bend and saw the mismatched boards of Josiah's shack in the small clearing. Just past the shack sat Uncle Owen's boat, surrounded by wispy cypress saplings on the log mooring down by the water. At the swamp's edge stood the wall of trees that we would wind our way through to get into the Okefenokee.

Uncle Owen pulled the wagon alongside the shack, and we both jumped down. While he tied up Selly, I moved my toes around in the dusty dirt, glad that my school shoes were back at home under my bed.

"Elsie Mae, why don't ya head down to the boat," Uncle Owen said, "while I go inside to git what's on Grandma's list. I won't be more'n a minute. Bear's down there waitin' for ya."

"Ya brought Bear?"

Uncle Owen winked at me and headed toward the porch steps. I grabbed my flour sack with my packed belongings and walked toward the landing.

"Hey there, Bear," I called, and Bear sleepily lifted his head. But as soon as I dropped my flour sack and patted my knees, Bear stood up and shook himself awake.

He barked "hello" and climbed out of the boat. He got more excited as he trotted toward me, and by the time he was close enough for me to pet him, he barked and danced around like I was his favorite person in the world. I couldn't wait to have a dog just like him.

I kneeled and rubbed his ears and buried my face in his neck. I loved all of Uncle Owen's dogs, but Bear was my favorite.

"C'mon, Bear," I said as I picked up my bag.

We walked toward the swamp's edge and stepped into Uncle Owen's boat. It wobbled a bit and sank some in the shallow water of the swamp's edge.

Bear settled himself into a comfortable spot to sleep again, and I sat down next to my bag and crossed my legs. I knew Uncle Owen would be more than just a minute. He and Josiah would most likely get to talking, and it might be a whole bunch of minutes before he was ready to leave.

"How 'bout pretendin' to be the president?" I asked, looking at Bear.

Bear didn't pick up his head, but he looked at me with his eyes. He was the only audience I had, so he'd have to do.

I reached into my pocket and pulled out the letter, smoothing out the wrinkles.

May 29, 1933

Dear Mr. President Roosevelt,

My name's Elsie Mae, and I live in Waycross, Georgia.

Other night when my uncle Owen was over for supper, he told us about a ship company that wants to build a canal right through the Okefenokee Swamp. Uncle Owen says something like that could just about ruin the swamp.

And then he said, "About the only person I can think of that could stop it'd be the president himself."

That's when I decided to write you this letter.

I wish you could come to the swamp, Mr. President. If you did, I'd take you out in Uncle Owen's boat, and we'd pole between the tall, skinny trees that grow right up out of the water and paddle across lakes full of lily pads. Then I'd make you lie down in the boat and look straight up at the sky and just listen. If you did that, Mr. President, you'd know that what my uncle Owen *says is true. "The Okefenokee is just a little piece of heaven on earth."*

That's why someone has to stop that ship company from building that canal.

I hope that someone is you!

Sincerely,
Elsie Mae Marshall

When my teacher wrote an A on the paper, she also wrote:

Elsie Mae, I've never seen you write so much for an assignment.

She was right about that. I usually wrote as little as I could get by with.

It's quite ambitious of you to think of writing to the president.

Ms. Jameson

Sending the letter wasn't part of the assignment, but I

knew even before Ms. Jameson graded it that I would send it. So, I had copied the letter over in my best penmanship, and that was what I had just mailed to President Roosevelt. And if my letter really *did* convince the president to stop that ship company, it meant that the Okefenokee would be saved.

It also meant that Mama and Daddy might start doing more than just a little bit of bragging on me.

Chapter 3

"We're gittin' close to the place where yer daddy and me got baptized," Uncle Owen said as he pushed and pulled at the swampy ground with his long, forked stick, moving the flat, wooden boat through the shrubs that covered the surface of the water.

It had been an hour or so since we'd left Josiah's, and I sat on my bag in the middle of the boat. Bear lay sleeping in the front, and Uncle Owen stood in the back.

As we traveled a tunnel-like path of tall, skinny pine and cypress trees, we had already seen eleven snakes, a doe and her fawn, a school of otter that made Bear bark like crazy, eight gators, and more egrets and herons than I could count. The channel widened little by little, letting more and more light seep in, and I could feel the water underneath the boat getting deeper and deeper.

"Why'd ya git baptized way up here?" I asked. "There's lotsa ponds and lakes closer to where ya lived."

"Had no choice," Uncle Owen said, putting down his forked stick to pick up the long wooden paddle that lay on the bottom of the boat. "This is as far as the preacher would come. We done it right over there in that cove," he said, pointing.

Uncle Owen continued, "I r'member thinkin' as the preacher dunked my head underwater that I needed more savin' from the gators in the swamp than I needed savin' from my sins."

He chuckled.

"There was gators 'round when ya did it?" I asked.

"There was gators all over the place, Elsie Mae," Uncle Owen answered. "Ya know Grandpa's friend Hamp? There was so many gators back then that the two of 'em kilt forty-two in one night."

My skin grew clammy just thinking about the danger. Gators and snakes lurking around every twist and turn of the swamp. It must've been awful exciting. There were still a lot of critters in the Okefenokee, but I knew there were nowhere near as many as when my daddy and Uncle Owen were growing up.

"But those good ol' days might could be as good as gone," Uncle Owen said.

"What do ya mean?" I asked.

"That ship company. Ya know, the one I was telling yer pa about last month when I was up at yer house fer supper?"

"Yes, sir," I answered.

"Josiah jus' tol' me t'day that some fella who's supposedly seen the plans fer the canal come by the other day and tol' him jus' how big the thing's gonna be," Uncle Owen explained. "Somethin' that size is gonna tear up the swamp somethin' fierce. Don't know how much longer…"

His voice trailed off, and he didn't finish what he was saying.

"Maybe it won't be as bad as folks think," I offered.

Uncle Owen stopped paddling and turned to me. "Elsie Mae, the water's the lifeblood of this swamp. Man tries to control it, there ain't no tellin' what might happen."

Then he sighed.

"Yer pa's got the right idea, movin' into Waycross and making a different kinda life fer you kids. The swamp's in danger this time. It's a real shame."

Uncle Owen moved his paddle again in that rhythmic way that looked more like he was conducting the church choir than guiding a boat through the swamp. He looked as though his thoughts had floated off somewhere above the highest branches of the tallest cypress trees that swayed in the breeze. I couldn't imagine Uncle Owen living anywhere but the Okefenokee. Swamp life was in his blood. It was in mine too.

I hoped with every drop of the swamp blood in my body that, by some miracle, my letter would be enough to save the Okefenokee for all of us, because if it was, I wouldn't just be giving Mama and Daddy a reason to be proud of me, I'd most likely be a big, huge hero for the rest of my life.

We finally reached the place called the Big Water, and the boat glided out into the wide-open smoothness of the tea-colored swamp. I leaned back on my elbows and tipped my head toward the big, blue Okefenokee sky. Even though we'd already been traveling for a couple hours, we had several more to go, so I closed my eyes, letting the sun hit my face. The heat of midday pressed against my skin, and I swatted the air, fighting off the pesky yellow flies that buzzed my head, but I found myself bothered by more than just bugs. There was no way to wave away that bad feeling I got in my stomach when I thought about how worried Uncle Owen sounded about that ship company building that canal. And even peskier than that was the thought that maybe my letter *wouldn't* be enough to make a difference. Maybe Mama was right. Maybe it was just plain foolishness for an eleven-year-old girl to think she could become a hero by writing a letter to the White House.

~ ❋ ~

The next thing I knew, Uncle Owen was shaking my shoulder.

"C'mon, Elsie Mae," he said, "better git yerself a drink 'fore ya git too thirsty."

I propped myself up on my elbow. My damp bangs stuck to my forehead, and a trickle of sweat dripped from my neck down the center of my back. I was sweating worse than one of Grandpa Zeke's hogs.

"How long've I been asleep?" I asked.

"Oh, 'bout a good hour now. Must be all that studyin' ya been doin' in school," Uncle Owen said, winking.

He reached his hand over the side of the boat into the water and drew fast circles, making a tiny whirlpool. Then he leaned over the side of the boat, put his lips to the surface, and sucked water right out of the swamp.

"Ahhhh," he said. "There jus' ain't nothin' like it!"

He wiped his hand across his mouth and then rubbed it on the side of his overalls.

I swirled my hand in the water the same way, leaned over the boat, and took a good, long drink.

Uncle Owen had taught me on my very first trip to the Okefenokee how to make a gator hole to get a good, cool drink even on a hot day. And he was right. It was just so satisfying. Made me wish I could've sent the president a little bit of Okefenokee water with that letter, because if he could've tasted it, he'd want to save the swamp for sure.

I reached over and made a gator hole for Bear, and he leaned over the boat next and lapped up a mess of water. He drank more than Uncle Owen and me put together.

"Do ya want me to paddle fer a while?" I asked.

"And what am I gonna do?" Uncle Owen asked, standing up again. "Darn my socks?"

Even though he had been the one who taught me how to use his boat a couple summers ago, during our trips to Honey Island, he had never let me pole the boat.

"You jus' sit back and relax," he said, "and think 'bout the big surprise that's waitin' on ya when we git there."

"What surprise?" I asked.

"Oh, the one yer Uncle Lone and I have waitin' fer ya at Grandma and Grandpa's."

Uncle Lone was Daddy's youngest brother. He and Uncle Owen were the only ones in the family besides Grandma and Grandpa who still lived in the swamp. Uncle Lone was kind of a cranky sort, so I couldn't imagine why he would be in on a surprise for me.

"Can ya give me a clue?" I asked.

"Only that yer gonna love it," Uncle Owen answered.

"That's not a clue," I said.

"Well, take it or leave it. It's the only clue yer gittin'," he said with a sly grin on his face.

Chapter 4

"Yeeeeowwwweeee! Yeeeowwwweee!"

The sound woke me from a deep sleep. My head lay against my flour-sack bag, and my cheek lay on the back of my hand, which was now full of drool. I sat up, wiped the drool on my overalls, and rubbed my eyes.

Uncle Owen's swamp call meant we were close to Honey Island. He had hollered to let Grandma and Grandpa know that we were almost home. I sat up in the boat. It was dark, but there was a full moon, and its light sneaked through the trees making the water look almost bright. Even so, I had no idea how Uncle Owen could find his way through the swamp at night. With as many summers as I'd spent in the Okefenokee, I had a hard time finding my way even in the daylight. In the dark, I knew I was sure to get lost.

Before we even reached the island, I could hear Uncle Owen's other dogs barking. Bear barked back to them, and when we got close enough, I could see Grandma Sarah and Grandpa Zeke standing on the landing waiting for us. The closer we got, the more Bear barked and barked as if he wanted to tell Grandma and Grandpa and the other dogs all about our trip.

Finally, Uncle Owen slid the boat up onto the soggy swamp's edge, and as soon as I felt the ground underneath us, I stood up.

"Why, Elsie Mae!" Grandma Sarah exclaimed. "Ya must've growed an inch or more since our visit up to yer place a coupla months ago."

"She looks more like her Grandma Sarah every time I see her," Grandpa Zeke said proudly.

Grandma and Grandpa loved fussing over me. They were proud of me just for growing. No wonder I love my swamp summers so much.

I carefully made my way along the bottom of the boat.

"Hi, Grandma and Grandpa," I said, getting out and hugging them.

They both felt smaller, but as I looked around in the bright moonlight, I saw that the landing at Honey Island hadn't changed a bit since last summer. And even though from down here at the swamp's edge I couldn't yet see the cabin, I could smell the two chinaberry trees that grew on either side of the gate in the front yard. I took a deep breath, letting it all sink in.

Gatordog, Hounder, Boondock, and Otter ran around me, sniffing and barking and making sure I said hello to them too. And even though I didn't see Uncle Lone anywhere, his dog named Dog was there. I reached down and petted each one on the head, and Bear ran back and forth along the shore so glad for the chance to be back with his dog brothers.

As Uncle Owen got out of the boat and pulled it all the way out of the water, the dogs barked and pranced in a frenzy of friendliness to see him. He grabbed each one of their heads and gave an affectionate rub, which only made them bark louder.

They loved Uncle Owen as much as I did. Most swampers treated their dogs well, especially if they were good hunters, but Uncle Owen treated his dogs better than anybody in the whole Okefenokee. Uncle Lone was just the opposite. He was cranky and cross with Dog, and I kind of wondered if the reason Dog wasn't a very good hunter was because of Uncle Lone's orneriness. I also wondered if Dog might even be a little bit jealous of Uncle Owen's dogs.

"Ya made good time," Grandpa said over the baying dogs.

"Yeah," Uncle Owen said, reaching down to grab my bag, "Not bad."

"Y'all must be starved," Grandma said. "C'mon up to the house, and we'll git ya somethin' to eat."

At the mention of food, my stomach growled like a hunting dog. That afternoon, Uncle Owen and I had eaten the mess of peanuts and peaches Mama had sent with us, but even so, I was starved.

Uncle Owen gave a quick whistle, piercing the night air, and the dogs calmed down as if he'd put a spell on them. They stood at Uncle Owen's side in silence looking up at him. And when he snapped his fingers and pointed toward his boat, they all trotted over, climbed in one after the other, and each found a place to settle down and sleep.

"I'll come back fer 'em after we eat," he said.

So the four of us left the dogs and walked up the trail toward the yard, and just before we got there Grandpa said, "I know y'all are hungry, but Elsie Mae might want to git to her surprise 'fore she eats."

Grandma had her arm around me, and she squeezed my shoulder.

"Oh yeah!" I exclaimed, feeling curiosity fill my growling stomach with excitement. "Uncle Owen tol' me there was some kinda surprise waitin' on me, but he wouldn't even give me a clue."

I looked over my shoulder at Uncle Owen with pretend scorn as we continued to walk.

"How's this fer a clue?" he asked, pointing straight ahead.

I looked up past the front gate to see Uncle Lone sitting in one of the rocking chairs on Grandma and Grandpa's front porch. I was confused. Uncle Lone was my surprise?

"Hi, Uncle Lone," I called.

"Don't 'hi' me," he said. "Git on up here and start takin' care of yer dog."

"My *dog*?" I asked.

And that's when I saw a dog sleeping on the porch next to Uncle Lone's feet.

"Yeah, this animal is 'bout as useless as a bag of chicken feed, which was what I was gonna tie 'round his neck when I drowned 'im."

"Oh, Lone," Grandma scolded as Grandpa held open the front gate so we could all walk through. "Stop that nasty talk. There ain't nothin' wrong with that dog."

We were all up on the porch now, and I knelt by the dog, who looked a lot different from the other hunting dogs. He lifted his sleepy head to look at me.

I still didn't understand what was going on.

"Yer givin' me this dog?" I asked, looking up at Uncle Lone and then back at Uncle Owen.

"That's right," Uncle Lone said, "and with good riddance. I found 'im a coupla weeks ago over near Cravens Hammock. He must've been in a real mess of a fight. Look at that big ol' scar under his neck."

I tipped the dog's head back and looked at the folds of skin underneath him. I couldn't imagine what could've happened to leave such a lumpy scar.

"He's been nothin' but a nuisance ever since I took 'im in. He won't mind, and he gets into nothin' but trouble. 'Sides that, somethin's gotta be wrong with 'em cuz I ain't never heard a peep outta him—not so much as a bark, yip, or growl. Just ain't normal, if ya ask me."

"Now ya know how we felt raisin' you," Grandpa Zeke said. "'Cept of course fer the keepin' quiet part. We all know ya couldn't talk less if ya tried."

Everyone laughed—everyone except Uncle Lone. Uncle Owen laughed the hardest.

"Ya mean I git to keep 'im? For real? Forever?" I exclaimed.

"Yep," Uncle Owen answered, "I talked it over with yer daddy this morning. It took some convincin', but he had to agree. He might be older than me, but he knows I could still beat 'im in a fight."

Uncle Owen grinned.

I couldn't believe it!

I had wanted a dog for as long as I could remember, but Mama and Daddy always said, "Last thing this family needs is one more thing that needs feedin'. Certainly not a dog!"

"What's his name?" I asked, petting his head.

"I jus' call 'im Brown," Uncle Lone said, "but he don't come when I call 'im, so it really don't matter what his name is."

The dog was tan, and he was medium-size, with long, droopy ears. His skin was sort of saggy, almost as if he was wearing a coat that was too big for him. He had a long nose and big, sad eyes. He kind of looked like I should feel sorry for him, and knowing how ornery Uncle Lone could be *did* make me feel sorry for him.

"Well, since he don't know his name," I said, "maybe I'll give him a new one."

"Now there's an idea!" Grandpa said.

"Don't matter what name ya give 'im," Uncle Lone piped in. "He's still not gonna mind ya."

"Oh, Lone, hush up!" Grandma scolded.

I scratched the dog's ears, and he let out a long sigh.

"So what're ya gonna name 'im, Elsie Mae?" Grandma asked.

"Don't know yet," I said. "I'll wait till I git to know 'im a little. Then I'll pick out the perfect name."

"That sounds like a dandy idea," Grandpa said.

"Well, what's there to eat 'round here, Ma?" Uncle Owen asked. "I'm 'bout as hungry as a hog who missed supper."

"I made some of Elsie Mae's favorites," Grandma said. "Snap beans and squash, boiled rice and pork gravy, baked sweet potatoes, and fried bacon with cornbread. It's all warmin' in the oven."

"And there's huckleberry pie fer dessert," Grandpa added. "I been dyin' fer a piece of that all day, but Sarah wouldn't let me have so much as a crumb till y'all showed up."

Grandma's huckleberry pie was my favorite of favorites, and everyone else's too.

"Well, let's stop talkin' 'bout it and git at it then," Uncle Owen said, opening the screen door.

Everyone filed inside, and I kissed my new dog on the

top of his head. I wished I could've stayed out on the porch with him a little longer, but my hunger and Grandma's cooking were getting the best of me. I'd eat as fast as I could so I could hurry back out on the porch to sit with my new dog. Maybe Grandma would even let me bring him something to eat.

Chapter 5

That night after our late supper, Uncle Owen, Uncle Lone, and all their dogs left for home. They lived in their own cabin on the other side of Honey Island. It wasn't far, but still I always marveled at how they could find their way in the dark.

Whenever I asked them how they did it, they said, "Same way the fish and the birds know their way 'round."

It didn't make sense to me. It had taken me three whole summers to learn my way around well enough to go out in Uncle Owen's boat by myself. And even so, if I was planning to go far, I always took one of his dogs with me just in case. Now I'd be able to take my own dog.

Uncle Owen always used to joke that a dog makes a better partner than most men. "Yer dog always has yer best interest in mind. With people, ya never really know."

Even though it was late, Grandma and Grandpa let me stay out on the front porch with my new dog for a long time after our supper. I scratched his head and rubbed his ears. After a while he rested his head in my lap, and I felt his lumpy scar press into my legs. I wondered what could've happened to him. I wondered if the scar had anything to do with why he didn't bark or growl or yip, but it really didn't matter to me. Even with his big, lumpy scar and no voice to bark or growl, I could already tell this dog was something special.

The long day and my full stomach made my body hum like the insects that filled the evening air. I rested myself on my dog's back and felt my eyelids grow heavier and heavier. Finally, Grandma took me by the shoulders and guided me inside. And the same way Uncle Owen and Uncle Lone could find their way home in the darkness of the swamp, I found my way to bed. I was half-asleep, but I somehow climbed the ladder to the loft where the bed Grandma had made for me waited.

— ❋ —

"Elsie Mae!" Grandma Sarah yelled. "Git on down here! Quick!"

I sat up in bed, first of all wondering where I was, and

second of all wondering what in the world was going on. Once I remembered I was up in Grandma and Grandpa's loft, I looked around for my overalls. Then I realized I still had them on. I must've been so tired that I slept in my clothes.

"Lord, have mercy! You go on, ya little rascal. Now git!"

Grandma Sarah was on a rampage. I couldn't imagine what was going on.

I jumped out of bed and started down the loft ladder to see Grandma chasing my new dog around the table and swatting at him with a dishrag.

"How'd he git in here?" I exclaimed.

"Must've pried that screen door open and snuck in," Grandma said, sounding out of breath.

I jumped off the loft ladder from the third rung and tried to cut my dog off at the pass by going around the table the other way, but he scooted under the table, escaping both of us. Once on the other side, he crawled under Grandma and Grandpa's bed at the far end of the room. Then he peeked out from under the edge of the quilt that hung down and looked up at me with purple drool dripping off his snout. That's when I noticed the empty pie tin in front of the stove.

"That darned dog ate every last crumb of the leftover pie," Grandma said, using the dishrag to wipe her forehead.

"Sorry, Grandma," I said, walking over to the bed to kneel by my dog. "He probly thought it smelled so good, he jus' had to have a taste."

"Oh, it's all right, I suppose," Grandma said, reaching down to pick up the pie tin. "No harm done, I guess, 'cept that yer grandpa's gonna be lookin' fer a piece of that pie 'round noon t'day."

I knew Grandma was right. Last night after supper, as I sat on the porch with my dog, even though I was full to bursting with that extra piece of cornbread I'd eaten and that double-size piece of huckleberry pie Grandma had given me, I had thought to myself about how good a leftover piece of pie would taste after my dinner the next day.

"How 'bout I git ya more huckleberries t'day, and ya can make 'nother pie?" I offered.

"Yer a good girl," Grandma said, ruffling my hair. "That'd be jus' fine, but ya better git that dog outta this house 'fore yer grandpa comes in fer his breakfast."

Grandma was so much quicker to forgive than Mama was.

"I will," I said, "but ya know what?"

"What?" Grandma asked, wiping her forehead again before walking back over to the sink to wash out the tin.

"I'm gonna call 'im Huck," I said proudly.

"Why that's a perfect name, Elsie Mae," Grandma said. "It suits 'im jus' fine."

Grandma Sarah was right. The name did suit him fine, especially with his huckleberry-stained snout.

"C'mon, Huck," I said, leading him out the screen door. "Let's go out on the porch and wait fer Grandpa."

Chapter 6

As I sat outside on the porch rubbing Huck's head and scratching his ears, I looked up and saw Uncle Owen and Uncle Lone coming through the gate.

"Where're the dogs?" I asked as they walked between the two chinaberry trees.

"Back at our place," Uncle Owen said, his shoes scuffing up the wooden steps of the porch. "Lone and I've got some catchin' up t'do on work 'round our place. We're headed back right after we eat, so we left 'em there."

"Yer the one's got the catchin' up t'do. I've been here all 'long workin'," Uncle Lone grumbled.

He shook his head and muttered to himself, "Takin' two days to go on up to Waycross to git Elsie Mae. I woulda made JD bring her down. It'd do that brother of ours some good to git outta that store of his and leave Waycross fer a change. He might remember what real work looks like."

"Don't ya ever git tired of bein' cross?" Uncle Owen asked, reaching for the screen door. "Ya yip more than a huntin' dog that jus' chased a coon up a tree."

"Least I do my share," Uncle Lone yipped back, following Uncle Owen inside.

"*You* stay here," I said to Huck as I got up to follow them.

"You boys better not be makin' a ruckus already this early in the mornin'," Grandma said as she set a plate of steaming biscuits on the table right next to the grits. "Where's yer pa?" she asked, goin' back to the stove to git more food. "Eggs are gittin' cold."

"Had to go over to Hamp's place this mornin'," Uncle Owen answered. "'Nother one of his hogs is missin'."

"Heavens!" Grandma exclaimed, turning around and putting her hands on her hips. "Not again."

"Hogs?" I asked as I slid onto the bench on the far side of the table to sit next to Uncle Owen.

"Seems we've got ourselves some hog bandits in these parts," Uncle Owen said.

"What do ya mean hog bandits?" I asked.

"He means a coupla scoundrels goin' 'round stealin' hogs," Uncle Lone explained as he sat down across from Uncle Owen and me. "And I aim to be the one to find 'em, and when I do, they'll be sorry they ever stepped foot in our swamp."

"Lone! Hush up with all that threatenin' talk," Grandma said, giving Uncle Lone one of her looks. "Yer gonna scare Elsie Mae with all this hog bandit business."

Then she turned to me.

"Now, Elsie Mae, don't ya trouble yerself with all this," she said, patting me on the shoulder. "There ain't nothin' to be 'fraid of."

"Not unless yer a hog," Uncle Lone said, scraping his bench on the floor as he scooted closer to the table.

"Enough, Lone!" Grandma scolded.

"Here," she said, handing him a biscuit. "Maybe that'll keep ya quiet."

Uncle Lone took the biscuit and shoved the whole thing in his mouth, and Grandma shook her head.

"Ya'd think I never taught 'im any manners," she said, turning directly to me as she sat down in the chair at the end of the table.

"Ma, we might as well fill Elsie Mae in on what's goin' on 'round here with the hog bandits," Uncle Owen said, ignoring his brother's ill-mannered behavior. "She's gonna be hearin' 'bout stuff."

I grabbed a biscuit from the basket, broke off a piece, and popped it into my mouth. I looked at Grandma to see if she agreed with Uncle Owen.

"Well, all right, but I don't want you boys frightenin' her."

I turned to Uncle Owen.

"Fer a coupla months now," he began, "folks've had their hogs come up missin'."

"But that's all, Elsie Mae," Grandma encouraged before he could fill in more of the details. "Nobody's been hurt."

"Nobody's been hurt?" exclaimed Uncle Lone, getting red in the face. "Ya think it don't hurt folks to lose one of their hogs!"

"Ya know what I mean, Elsie Mae," Grandma said, ignoring Uncle Lone's outburst. "They ain't never harmed anyone, jus' stolen."

"Jus' stolen…" Uncle Lone said under his breath. "Jus' wait. I'm gonna be the one to find those scoundrels, and when I do, everybody'll be thankin' me."

"How do ya know it's not a bear or a cougar stealin' the hogs?" I asked after swallowing a bite of eggs.

Uncle Owen smiled.

"Ya've learned a lot spendin' yer summers in the swamp, Elsie Mae. That's exactly what we suspected till we started noticin' that nobody ever found any hog parts lyin' 'round. Bears and cougars'll always leave a trail."

"Hmm," I said, thinking. "Well, how many hogs've been stolen?"

"Oh, I don't know," Uncle Owen said. "Altogether, folks've maybe lost 'bout ten or twelve or so."

"Thankfully we haven't lost a one," Grandma said, sounding relieved.

"And we ain't goin' to," Uncle Lone said. "Cuz we do, and I'll git my hands on those low-downs and wring their skinny little necks."

"Oh, Lone," Grandma said, "stop talkin' like you're addled in the brain. You'll do no such thing."

Uncle Lone grunted and stuffed another whole biscuit in his mouth. We all ate in silence for a few minutes.

"What's everybody gonna do 'bout it?" I finally asked.

"*Everybody's* gonna *talk* 'bout findin' 'em," Uncle Lone said in a singsongy, sweet tone.

Then he leaned forward and went on in his usual Uncle Lone tone, "But I'm actually gonna be the one t'do it. And when I do, folks 'round here should want to offer me some kinda reward or somethin' fer all my trouble."

He put a huge spoonful of eggs in his mouth, put his chin up in the air, and chewed with a prideful grin on his face.

"That's one of the things Pa's over at Hamp's fer right now," Uncle Owen said. "He wants to collect some money from folks 'round here fer a reward."

"Really!" Uncle Lone exclaimed with excitement, leaning forward again and almost choking on his big mouthful of eggs.

"That's what I heard Pa say to Farley when he come by to tell us 'bout their missin' hog," Uncle Owen explained.

"'Bout time," Uncle Lone said.

"And Farley tol' Pa that the other day when Sheriff Jones come by their place," Uncle Owen continued, "the sheriff said he's got his eyes and ears open in hopes of helpin' us find those bandits."

"Sheriff Jones," Uncle Lone grumbled. "That lunatic couldn't find water if he fell out of a boat. He's the last person we need helpin' us."

Uncle Lone had had a run-in with Sheriff Jones a couple years ago. I never knew on account of what, but it must've been something pretty bad because Uncle Lone had spent a little time in Folkston Prison on account of it. Ever since then, if anyone even mentioned Sheriff Jones—or any officer of the law, for that matter—Uncle Lone had something to say about it.

"Lone, you hush up, or I'm gonna give *you* what's for!" Grandma scolded. "Mark my words. That's my last warning!"

It was funny how even though he was all grown up, Uncle Lone still got in trouble from his mama. I smiled to myself, and Uncle Owen winked at me.

"I named my new dog this morning," I said, changing the subject to something more pleasant.

"Oh, yeah, what's that?" Uncle Lone said. "Twigs for brains?"

Boy, Uncle Lone was *really* in a bad mood this morning. He was always ornery, but this was worse than usual.

"Lone Marshall!" Grandma yelled. "Git yerself up offa that bench, and git yer sorry self outside. I've had 'bout enough of yer jibber-jabber this mornin'."

I covered my mouth, trying to hide my giggles, and Uncle Owen elbowed me as his shoulders shook with silent laughter. Uncle Lone pushed himself away from the table and got up. He dropped his dishes in the sink with a clatter and then let the screen door bang behind him.

"I don't know what gits into that boy sometimes," Grandma said, wiping her forehead with the dish towel that was lying in her lap.

"C'mon, Elsie Mae, I'm dyin' to hear the name," Uncle Owen said, leaning his shoulder into me.

"Huck," I said proudly. "On accounta Grandma catching him eatin' the leftovers of her pie this mornin'."

Uncle Owen's belly laugh filled the room, and when he stopped laughing, he said, "That sounds 'bout right."

I smiled.

"So I guess that means no leftover pie this afternoon?" Uncle Owen asked.

"Sorry," I said sheepishly.

"What're ya sorry 'bout? Not yer fault the dog's got good taste."

Uncle Owen pushed his end of the bench back and stood up. "Well, I better git back to our place and git some work done before Uncle Lone becomes all-out impossible to live with. Elsie Mae, you and Huck'll have to be on yer own t'day. Maybe by t'morrow I'll be caught up, and I can take some time off to take ya fishin'."

"Yes, sir," I said. "Huck and I are gonna pick some huckleberries fer Grandma so she can make another pie."

43

"Sounds fine," Uncle Owen said. "Help yerself to my boat if ya want. I won't be needin' it t'day."

"Elsie Mae, you be careful out in that boat," Grandma said, standing to clear the dishes. "I don't want anythin' happenin' to ya while yer under my care."

I didn't mind Grandma's worrying over me all summer. It was better than all the nagging and scolding that I knew was going on way up in Waycross at my house.

"Ma, she'll be fine," Uncle Owen said as he headed outside. "I taught her everythin' she needs to know 'bout the swamp," he called over his shoulder.

"Yeah, and 'sides," I said to Grandma, "now I have Huck to pal around with."

I looked out the screen door at Huck with his purple-stained snout lying in the shade on the porch, and when Grandma wasn't looking, I snuck a biscuit into my pocket to give him later.

Chapter 7

Once Uncle Owen left, I went outside to the front porch.

"C'mon, Huck," I said, holding the stolen biscuit toward him as I jumped down the porch steps and headed across the yard.

Huck hungrily and gratefully grabbed the biscuit, chewing as he followed me past the chinaberry trees and through the gate down the dirt trail to the water. It seemed he was already getting used to his new name.

Uncle Owen's boat lay in some brush up on the swamp's edge, right where we'd left it the night before. I swatted at the mosquitoes and flies buzzing around my head as I pushed the boat halfway out into the water. Then I stepped in and grabbed the long-forked pole that lay inside.

"Jump in, Huck," I said, motioning for him to join me in the boat.

But Huck's paws stood firm on the landing.

"C'mon, boy," I coaxed as I patted my legs. "Let's go!"

A breeze blew through the trees, and Huck almost seemed to shake his head "no" as he dug his toenails into the dirt. I wondered if somehow he knew that Uncle Lone had thought about drowning him. If it wasn't for Uncle Owen thinking about giving him to me, Huck would've never tasted Grandma's huckleberry pie. He would've been swimming to save his life.

Just thinking about what could've happened to Huck sent a shiver down my spine, even though the back of my neck already felt sticky with sweat.

"It's OK, boy!"

Huck sat down, wiggled his rear end deeper into the dirt, and looked at me with his long, sad face. I realized he was never going to get in by himself. I tossed the pole on the ground and stepped out of the boat. Then I picked up Huck's front paws and walked him on his hind legs toward the boat. His front claws dug into the palms of my hands, and his breath, which didn't smell as sweet as that huckleberry pie he'd just eaten, warmed my neck. I breathed out of my mouth as he drooled on my shirt.

"Don't worry, Huck," I said. "I gotcha."

I stepped into the boat backward, still holding Huck's paws, and the boat wiggled and wobbled. Huck's expression got even sadder, and his nails dug deeper into my hands. Even so, I kept pulling him toward me anyway, but as I did, the wobbling got worse, until we both fell to the bottom of the boat, rocking it back and forth. Huck scratched and clawed, trying to get himself right ways up again.

"Easy, Huck," I said. "Easy."

I rolled over, wiping away the dog slobber that had splashed onto my face. I sat up, trying to keep the boat steady. All the while, I held on to a handful of skin on Huck's neck with one hand as he clawed at the bottom of the boat. I slowly stood up, keeping one foot on either side of him.

Now I needed to get the pole to push us out into the water. It was still up on the landing. I let go of Huck's neck with my hand and tightened the grip on his rear end with my legs and feet. I crouched down, and the boat swiveled. I could feel Huck's heart pounding through his thick skin. Steadying myself, I walked my hands along the shore. I stretched as far as I could and reached the pole. I stood up slowly, still keeping a tight grip on Huck with my feet.

"Here we go, Huck," I said.

I pushed hard on the pole to move the boat away from Honey Island. We rocked back and forth a little, but then smoothly floated out into the deeper tea-colored water of the swamp.

For a while Huck sat between my legs, still nervous and stiff, but as we drifted farther and farther into the swamp, I felt his heartbeat slow down and his body relax. He watched the egrets that stood in the shallow water catching fish. We saw three deer in the woods and a gator sunning itself on a log and another one lying in the shallow waters of the prairie south of Honey Island, but Huck didn't seem scared anymore. And finally, he stretched himself out, put his head on his front paws, and fell asleep.

I looked around and took a deep breath. Here I was, not only in my favorite place in the whole world, doing one of my favorite things, but I was here doing it with my very own dog. Now if only, by some miracle, my letter to President Roosevelt could convince him to stop that ship company from building that canal, there'd be nothing else that could make this summer more perfect.

Chapter 8

Huck and I spent the whole morning in Uncle Owen's boat. Then at noon Grandma and I ate our dinner out on the porch together because Grandpa wasn't back yet, and Uncle Owen and Uncle Lone were still getting caught up on work over at their place.

Once Grandma went back inside to clean up, Huck and I headed to the other side of Honey Island to the huckleberry patch for some picking. While I picked, Huck and I ate so many huckleberries I thought the two of us would just about burst. And when Grandma saw us heading up the porch steps with two baskets of berries, she laughed and laughed when she got a good look at us because Huck and I were as purple as a pile of huckleberries.

By the time we sat down for supper, Huck was so worn

out and his belly so full of berries that he fell fast asleep on the front porch. He was sleeping so hard I almost thought I heard him snoring.

"So, Elsie Mae, how's yer first day back in the swamp?" Grandpa asked as he sat in the chair at the head of the table.

"Great, sir!" I said as Grandma brought more food from the stove over to the table. "Huck and I went all the way 'round the island this mornin' in Uncle Owen's boat, and then after dinner we picked all those huckleberries for Grandma."

I pointed to the overflowing baskets next to the sink.

"Yeah, I do have a hankerin' fer more pie," Grandpa said, "and rumor is the leftovers is gone." He winked at me.

"Sorry 'bout that, Grandpa," I said.

Even though I knew he wasn't really mad, I still felt bad about the pie.

"But don't ya think Huck's a great name?" I asked, trying to put a positive spin on Huck's huckleberry incident.

"Sure do," Grandpa said, reaching for the spoon sticking out of the pork gravy.

"No problems with the boat then?" Uncle Owen asked as Grandma finally sat down in the chair opposite Grandpa.

"Well, not with the boat, but gittin' Huck in it wasn't 'specially easy," I said.

"That right," Uncle Owen said. "Probly jus' scared of water, I guess. And rightly so after what Lone was thinkin' of doin' to 'im."

"Don't ever bring that up again," Grandma scolded. "That boy can be so mean sometimes."

"Where is Uncle Lone t'night anyway?" I asked. "Why ain't he eatin' with us?"

"He's likely poutin'," Grandma said. "Always pouts for a day or two after I scold 'im like I did this mornin'."

"Yeah, when I got back to our place this mornin', he was already gone to who knows where. But no matter. Jus' means more biscuits fer us," Uncle Owen said, grabbing two out of the bread basket and dropping them in the gravy on his plate.

We all chewed in silence for a few minutes. Grandma's cooking didn't just taste good; it actually made you *feel* good inside. Mama was a good cook too, but there was just something even better about everything Grandma made.

This first day here in the swamp was why I loved my summers so much—freedom to do whatever I wanted all day and evenings around the table with Grandma and Grandpa and Uncle Owen who were always interested, in a good way, with how I spent my day.

"When I was up at Hamp's today, Sheriff Jones come by," Grandpa said, "and I'm 'fraid I heard some bad news."

"'Bout the hog bandits?" I asked excitedly.

I had been so busy with Huck all day that I had forgotten all about those hog bandits.

"'Fraid this news is even worse than the hog bandits," Grandpa continued. "Seems that canal project might jus' be slated to start even earlier than any of us was figurin' on."

My letter didn't even have a chance to make it to the White House yet. Was it already too late?

I swallowed hard. Uncle Owen looked at Grandpa, and his expression made me want to cry.

"Lord, have mercy," Grandma said. "What's wrong with these people tryin' to mess with God's handiwork? Can't they jus' leave well enough alone?"

"Guess they can stand to make a lot of money with this thing," Grandpa explained.

"Money!" Grandma exclaimed. "The water in this swamp is worth a lot more than money."

"What will happen if they build it?" I asked, looking over at Grandpa.

"Hard to tell," he answered. "But it'll change everythin' 'bout the swamp—the huntin', the fishin', the plant life. Ya can't go messin' 'round with nature and not disrupt a lot of things."

"You've seen what that loggin' company did to Billys Island," Uncle Owen said.

I *had* seen it. The Hebard Lumber Company had cut down so many trees that parts of the swamp looked like a wasteland.

"Yes, sir, but the trees are growin' back," I said, trying to sound hopeful. "Right?"

"The water's different, Elsie Mae," Grandpa said. "The water's the heart of the swamp. If they mess with that, it may jus' be the end."

The end of the Okefenokee? I couldn't think of anything worse than that.

My letter was even more important than I had thought. If only there was some way to make sure the president really paid attention to it when it arrived, then it might have a chance to make the difference we all needed it to make.

Chapter 9

That night I lay up in the loft on top of the covers. The warm, thick air closed in around me, and the lingering smoke from Grandma's nightly oak-bark fire lay against my skin like a hazy blanket, keeping the mosquitoes away. The two rocking chairs that stood next to the mantel downstairs creaked back and forth in rhythm with the crickets outside. Grandma and Grandpa talked in hushed tones so as not to keep me awake.

I tried to listen to their conversation but couldn't make out enough words to know exactly what they were talking about, so my mind drifted back to our suppertime conversation. My imagination filled with big, heavy ships pushing their way straight through the new wide, canal-size waterways of the swamp. I pictured steam from those ships closing in on

Grandma and Grandpa's front porch as if it were a storm of fog coming in off the sea.

As worried as I was about that ship canal, I was worn out from my day with Huck and all the huckleberry picking. Those huge, heavy ships pulled at me through the gray, steamy fog of my dreamy imagination, steering me toward a big, drowsy island of sleep. But just before I slipped behind the foggy clouds of slumber, I heard Uncle Lone's voice drifting up toward the front porch.

"If ya say 'hallelujah' *one* more time, Henry James, I'm gonna—"

"That's jus' yer hard heart talkin', Uncle Lone. I think ya probly need *more* hallelujahs, not less. Fact is, it's probly why the Lord sent me to ya."

What was Uncle Lone doing here this late at night? And who in the world was Henry James? That island of sleep I'd been headed for sank to the bottom of my imaginary swamp like a bag of boulders. Suddenly wide awake, I sat up in bed.

"What in tarnation is Lone doin' here?" Grandpa exclaimed, stopping the creaky rhythm of his rocking chair.

"Lord only knows with that boy," Grandma answered. "And he's not alone. Sounds like he said 'Henry James.' Ya don't think he's got Harry and Rhodie's son with him, do ya?"

Rhodie was Grandma's youngest sister, but she didn't live in the Okefenokee anymore, so I'd never met her *or* her family. The only time Grandma mentioned Rhodie was when she told stories about her being off on some crazy lark doing something that ended up with her needing help getting out from under a big, huge heap of trouble she'd gotten herself into.

I climbed out of bed and crept to the edge of the loft and peered through the smoky haze hanging in the air. Just then, Uncle Lone pulled the screen door back and walked into the house. A boy, dressed in a black Sunday suit that was about two sizes too small for him, walked in behind Uncle Lone. His scuffed-up, hard-soled black shoes made hollow sounds on the wooden floor of the cabin.

"Well, Ma!" Uncle Lone exclaimed. "Yer sister's crazy, ex-con, revival-lovin', Bible-thumpin', travelin' preacher husband has *really* done it this time!"

Uncle Lone turned and pointed to the boy who looked like he might just pop out of that suit it was so small.

"Lone, yer 'bout as ornery as they come," Grandma said, heading across the room. "Henry James!" she exclaimed as she smothered the boy in one of her warm, welcoming hugs.

"Hi, Aunt Sarah," I heard him say into her shoulder as Grandma squeezed him.

I worried that Grandma would squeeze so hard that Henry's suit would explode, and we'd all be blown to bits.

She finally let go of Henry James and pushed her arms out straight, holding him by the shoulders. "Lemme git a good look at ya," she said. "I bet it's been more'n two years since I've seen ya last."

"Looks like yer goin' be tall like yer daddy," Grandpa said, walking over and putting his arm around Henry's shoulder to give him a squeeze.

"Hallelujah, Uncle Zeke!" Henry James yelled at the top of his lungs. "I'm prayin' I'll be tall cuz I'm plannin' to be a preacher jus' like my daddy. It'll be a blessing to be able to see out over all the lost souls when I'm leadin' those tent meetin's."

A preacher? I thought it was bad enough that my brothers wanted to grow up to work in Daddy's store and my sisters all wanted to get married as soon as they were old enough. But this boy wanted to be a preacher?

"Humph." Uncle Lone sighed, plopping down in Grandpa's rocking chair. "Yer daddy bein' a preacher makes 'bout as much sense as me conductin' the church choir."

"Lone!" Grandma scolded, swatting him on the arm. "Ya better watch yerself!"

She put her face close to Henry's and said, "Don't pay

him no mind, Henry James. Lone's so ornery it addles his brain sometimes."

I felt like my brain was a little addled. Why was this boy here? And how long was he planning to stay?

"So what are ya doin' here, son?" Grandpa asked.

Finally, someone was asking a question that made some sense!

"That's what *I* wanted to know," Uncle Lone said, leaning forward in the rocking chair. "Earlier t'day, I left my boat at Camp Cornelia while I was runnin' my sugarcane syrup over to Traders Hill to do some swappin', and when I got back, I found him sittin' in the boat waitin' fer me. Said his daddy and mama's gone on some travelin' tent revival trip down in Florida fer the summer.

"Guess they paid some fella from Folkston to git Henry to one of us. The fella planned to bring him all the way over to our place, but while I was down the road a bit takin' care of a few things, the fella stopped up at the Hill. Well, he got to talkin' and spoutin' his mouth off 'bout what he was doin' with the boy, and someone tol' 'im I was a relative of Henry's and that my boat was sittin' over at Camp Cornelia. So the darn fool jus' left Henry there, and when I come back down to head home, there he was."

Grandma tsked, and an uncomfortable silence filled the room.

"Daddy wanted to bring me 'long on the travelin' tent revival trip with him and Mama. It's jus' that, um, that…" Henry stammered. "There wasn't enough money in the goodwill offerin' to pay fer all three of us to go," he finished in a rush.

"Well, that's jus' our blessing now, isn't it?" Grandma said, pulling Henry James close to her again.

Blessing? Henry James here at Grandma and Grandpa's all summer a blessing? This was *my* summer!

"Yes, ma'am," I heard Henry say, but his words were muffled in the folds of Grandma's dress. Good thing for Henry because it mostly hid the way his voice cracked when he agreed with her. That little crack made me wish I didn't feel as ornery as Uncle Lone about Henry James horning in on my perfect summer in the swamp.

It was one thing for *me* to be here for the summer. I *wanted* to get out of *my* house, but no matter what Henry James said about his mama and daddy *wanting* to take him with them on their traveling revival tour, I knew that with every inch of him that was stuffed inside that suit, he didn't believe it.

"Well now, how long ya figurin' yer folks'll be gone?" Grandpa asked.

"Well, they got 'nough money in the offerin' t'do the whole Florida circuit from Jacksonville to Miami—twenty-five meetin's in ten weeks. Do ya know how many souls Daddy's gonna save? Hallelujah!"

"Souls he's gonna save?" Uncle Lone grumbled. "That low-down oughta start with his own—"

"Lone, if ya don't stop that jibber-jabber, I'm gonna tan yer hide," Grandma scolded.

"I imagine you and Elsie Mae will git on well this summer," Grandpa said, changing the subject.

And that was the first time anyone noticed me kneeling at the edge of the loft and listening to the whole ruckus. By now the smoke, meant to clear the cabin of mosquitoes, had lifted, and as everyone glanced up at me, they could see me clear as day. I smiled, hoping that somehow this was all part of that ship-canal nightmare I had imagined earlier. Maybe somehow it wasn't really true that some preacher boy named Henry James was about to ruin my summer.

"C'mon down, Elsie Mae, and meet yer cousin," Grandma said. "I have a feelin' the two of ya will be fast friends in no time."

I knew I wasn't dreaming when I felt the wooden steps of the loft ladder on my bare feet, and I was definitely sure I was wide awake when Henry James stuck out his hand to shake mine and said, "Hallelujah, the Lord jus' sent me a friend!"

No wonder Uncle Lone had been hollering about all the hallelujahs. I'd only just laid eyes on Henry James, but already he'd managed to squeeze three of his holy hallelujahs into the conversation. If this boy thought we were going to be friends, he was going to have to think again. I couldn't change the fact that we were relatives and that the both of us would be here all summer, but I sure didn't have to like it. And I didn't have to pal around with him either.

I had Huck.

And Huck and I didn't need Henry James *or* his hallelujahs.

Chapter 10

The next morning, by the time I climbed down from the loft, Grandma was the only one left inside.

"Well, we wasn't sure ya was ever gonna git up this mornin'," Grandma said when she heard my feet hit the floor. "I think that new dog of yers is wearin' ya out this summer, Elsie Mae, isn't he?"

"Yes, ma'am, he is," I said, hooking the left strap of my overalls.

I looked out the screen door, but didn't see Huck lying on the porch in the place that had already become his favorite.

"Where is everybody?" I asked. "And where's Huck?"

Grandma took the plates off the shelf above the sink and headed for the table.

"Well, if I know Huck, and I think I already do, he's

probly gittin' into somethin'. And Henry James and yer grandpa are out feedin' the hogs—all ten of 'em. Thankfully, they're all still safe and sound."

Oh yeah, Henry James. All that ruckus last night hadn't been a dream, and Henry James really *was* here. I looked over at the cot Grandma had fixed up for him in the corner opposite Grandma and Grandpa's bed and saw his scuffed-up shoes resting neatly against the wall.

"Why don't ya be a good girl and go on out and gather up the eggs fer me? I'm up to twenty-five chickens now, so ya know what that means. Plenty a eggs fer breakfast this summer, and maybe even some fried chicken some Sundays too."

"No wonder I love comin' here so much, Grandma," I said, smiling.

Grandma put her arm around me and squeezed.

"Once ya git those eggs, why dontcha call everyone to breakfast?" Grandma said. "The biscuits should be done real soon."

The biscuits smelled so good that I wasn't sure I could wait. That deliciousness had already floated up to the loft and was surely the reason I had woken up at all this morning.

"Are Uncle Lone and Uncle Owen comin' fer breakfast?" I asked.

"Not this mornin'," Grandma answered. "Uncle Lone's still fussin' over Henry James being here and says he's got business to take care of anyway. Don't know what business that boy could have 'cept the business of gittin' into trouble. And Uncle Owen left on an early-mornin' huntin' trip with Farley, one of Hamp's boys. He'll be gone most of the day. Now hurry up and go git those eggs fer me, Elsie Mae."

I headed outside and around back toward the barn and the chicken yard. I wanted to go over to the hog pen before I took care of the eggs and say good morning to Grandpa, but I looked across to the other side of the yard—past Grandma's garden, which had so much stuff growing in it that it looked more like a small farm than a garden—and saw Henry James. He was jabbering away at Grandpa while Grandpa tended the hogs.

I wasn't going over there if Hallelujah Henry was over there. I'd be seeing enough of him without going out of my way to see him even more.

I looked around the yard for Huck. I wondered where he could be, but I didn't have to wonder long. As soon as I pulled open the gate to the chicken yard, there he was.

"What're ya doin' in here, Huck?" I asked.

But as soon as I knelt to greet him with a nice firm

head rub and saw his gooey, yellow snout, I knew the answer to my question.

"Huck," I said in my sternest whisper, "are ya tryin' to git yerself in trouble?"

I grabbed a handful of his extra skin, banged open the chicken yard gate with my hip, and pulled Huck toward the pump. I pressed and pulled the handle up and down and then grabbed Huck's snout and stuck it under the trickle of water that came out. I splashed his nose and mouth and rubbed at the sticky, yellowy yolk while Huck tried to drink the water.

"Everyone was mad enough 'bout you eatin' that pie," I said, warning Huck. "What're they gonna say if they know yer out here eatin' the eggs?"

I'd have to be sure from now on that the chicken-yard gate was latched tight, or Grandma might start scoldin' Huck and me the way she did Uncle Lone.

Huck looked at me with that sad, lonely face that made me love him even more than I thought I could love a dog. I sighed.

"Jus' promise those'll be yer last eggs, and it'll be our secret," I said, rubbing his head and making a pact with him. "Now, I gotta go gather what's left. You stay here."

I turned around, and there was Henry James. He was

still wearing that too-small suit, but now he was barefoot, so the pants looked even shorter. The look on Henry's face told me that my and Huck's secret wasn't really a secret anymore.

"Ya know what the scriptures say: 'Be sure yer sins'll find ya out.'"

Was this how it was gonna be? Henry James sneaking up on me sprinklin' scripture around like it was chicken feed? I glared at him the way I did when my sisters told on me. And then I marched past him without saying a word. I flung open the gate to the chicken yard, wishing I could've punched Henry in the arm as hard as that gate banged against the fence. I grabbed the basket hanging on the hook attached to the coop, and as I reached for the first egg, I heard Grandma yell, "Breakfast!" And I saw Henry James run off toward the house.

Trying hard to hurry, but trying even harder to be careful, I gathered the eggs as quickly as I could. With a few already missing because of Huck's morning meal, I needed to be sure to safely deliver all the eggs that were left, or Grandma might get suspicious.

By the time I got back up to the house, Grandma, Grandpa, and Henry were all sitting at the table waiting for me.

As I opened the screen door, I heard Grandpa saying,

"We're gonna have to see if Owen or Lone has an old pair of overalls fer ya, Henry. Ya can't very well go 'round lookin' like that all summer."

"Yes, sir," Henry James said.

"Hope that basket is full this morning," Grandma said as she saw me coming in. "I've got some bakin' I want t'do."

I felt Henry's eyes on me almost like they was shooting flaming arrows of scripture at me.

"Jus' put the basket up next to the sink and skedaddle yerself 'round this table," Grandma said. "Yer grandpa's droolin' over these biscuits worse than that dog of yers."

I put up the eggs and then headed for the table. Henry gave me another knowing look as I sat down on the bench across the table from him.

Grandpa grabbed a biscuit as soon as I sat down, but Grandma's eyes gave him one of her silent scoldings—the kind of look she usually saved for Uncle Lone. And the kind of look she'd surely have given Huck, and maybe me too, if she knew what Huck had just done.

Grandpa stared at her as if she was as addled as Uncle Lone sometimes acted.

"Henry, would ya like to say grace fer us?" Grandma asked politely.

"Yes, ma'am," Henry James said.

Grandpa and I raised our eyebrows at each other.

Grandma, Grandpa, Uncle Owen, and Uncle Lone were churchgoers when there was a reverend preaching nearby, and I had seen Grandma reading her Bible lots of times, but in all the summers I'd stayed with them, we had never been in the habit of saying grace before meals. In fact, it was the only sore spot Mama had about me spending my summers in the swamp.

I'd overheard her say to Daddy once, "Well, I jus' wish they kept their hearts a li'l closer to the Lord, that's all. I don't want Elsie Mae comin' home a heathen."

"My family thinks God created the Okefenokee before he created anything else," Daddy joked. "I don't think ya can git more God-respectin' than that."

Mama had snorted at that and didn't sound at all convinced.

With Henry James here, Grandma must've felt we should make an effort to be a little more religious. But from the look Grandpa had just given me, he didn't seem to feel the same way. Even so, he let go of his biscuit, and we all bowed our heads and closed our eyes.

"Dear Lord," Henry began, "we come before ya with hearts full of sin…"

Hearts full of *sin*? Was Henry going to reveal Huck's wrongdoings in a prayer? Wasn't telling others about someone else's sin some kind of sin too?

I reached my foot under the table and felt around for Henry's foot with my big toe. When I felt it, I dug my toenail into the top of his foot. Thankfully my nail was just long enough to make him squirm.

"But we know ya fergive us fer all our transgressions, whether big or small; and we thank ya fer that," Henry said, changing his tone, "and fer this food. Amen!"

By the time any of us opened our eyes, Grandpa already had half a biscuit in his mouth.

"Zeke," Grandma scolded, "ya have no patience."

"Ya can't blame a man fer being hungry, Sarah," Grandpa said. "'Sides, how can I help myself when my wife makes the best biscuits in the entire Okefenokee?"

"Grandma makes the best *everything* in the entire Okefenokee," I said and chewed with a big smile on my face.

I wasn't just happy about eating one of Grandma's biscuits. I was happy that I had put Henry James in his place. He thought he could scare me with his preacher talk, but forget about the fear of God. Henry James hadn't even been here a whole day yet, and I'd already put a little fear of Elsie Mae in him.

Just as Grandma was scooping a big heap of eggs onto my plate, we all heard Uncle Lone's swamp call coming up from the water.

"*Yeeowwwweeoo! Yeeowwwweeoo!*"

"Now what in tarnation is that boy doin' here this mornin'?" Grandpa asked with his mouth full of his third biscuit.

"Lord only knows," Grandma said.

"When I pressed him on what he was doin' this mornin', he wouldn't give me no straight answer. He best not be out runnin' with that wild bunch he was runnin' with a coupla years ago. He gits himself in trouble again, and Sheriff Jones ain't gonna give him a break this time," Grandpa said.

"Zeke," Grandma scolded and shot Grandpa one of her looks.

I knew her look meant she didn't want Grandpa talking about Uncle Lone and the sheriff in front of Henry and me.

"What happened with the sheriff?" Henry asked.

"Oh, never ya mind," Grandma said, turning to Henry. "Nothin' fer ya to worry 'bout. Jus' pray fer yer Uncle Lone, would ya, Henry? He could use all the help he could git."

"Pa!" we heard Uncle Lone yell, sounding as if he was halfway up the trail to the house. "Pa!"

We all scooted away from the table and hurried out the door and onto the porch.

Uncle Lone was just inside the gate. "It's them hog bandits again, Pa! They done got four more hogs last night. Over at Hatcher's this time."

"Hog bandits!" Henry James exclaimed. "Who are *they*?"

Grandma put her arm around Henry and said, "Don't ya never mind 'bout them either, but ya might want to put the hogs on that prayer list of yers too."

"Prayer list!" Uncle Lone exclaimed, stomping up the porch steps. "Sittin' 'round prayin' 'bout it ain't gonna do no good. We need to set a trap and catch those low-downs so's we can throw 'em in the slammer. And that's exactly what I aim t'do."

Funny how Uncle Lone couldn't wait to get those hog bandits behind bars when he had ended up that way himself a while back. Maybe that made him the perfect one to catch the hog bandits since he was probably the most like them.

"What did y'all decide up at Hamp's the other day?" Uncle Lone asked, looking at Grandpa. "Owen said there might be some kinda reward."

"Well," Grandpa said. "We all decided we'd put some money up, and we collected fifty dollars. But Lex said, and rightly so, if we're plannin' to offer a reward, we need to let the sheriff hold the money, so there ain't no funny business 'bout who gits it."

"Well, ain't that nice," Uncle Lone said. "It'll be sweet justice when Sheriff Jones hands that money over to me when I find those low-downs."

"Most swamp folk I know likely wouldn't even accept no reward," Grandpa said.

"Well, I ain't *most folk*," Uncle Lone said. "And I *will* be acceptin' it."

Grandma shook her head and tsk-tsked.

"I can't stop ya from takin' the money. It's yer mind to make up, but I'll warn ya. Now that we're offerin' a reward, we might could have some outsiders comin' in here searchin' fer those bandits," Grandpa said. "Best we take some caution with that."

"There won't be no reason fer caution," Uncle Lone said smugly. "Jus' wait! I'll be findin' those bandits 'fore the next full moon. And swamp folk or not, I'll be takin' that reward money home myself, 'long with all the glory when this face," he said, pointing to himself, "is on the front page of the *Charlton County Caller* fer bein' a great big hero."

And with that, Uncle Lone stomped down the steps, through the gate, and back in the direction he'd come from.

As he walked away, Grandma and Grandpa both shook their heads.

"Would Uncle Lone really git his picture in the newspaper?" I asked.

"Suppose he might," Grandpa said. "But he's gotta find those hog bandits first."

That gave me an idea.

Maybe somehow *I* could solve the hog bandit mystery, and if I did, it could be *my* picture on the front page of the *Charlton County Caller* instead of Uncle Lone's. Not only would I get to be a great big hero for saving the hogs; if my picture *did* end up in the newspaper, I'd surely get to tell the story of how I found the hog bandits. And when I did, I'd somehow find a way to mention that I didn't just want to save the swamp from the hog bandits, but that I planned to save the entire Okefenokee with my letter to the White House. Maybe *that* would be the way to get the president to pay attention to my letter before it was too late to save the swamp.

Chapter 11

Later that day, on my way down to the landing, I heard Henry James's voice coming up through the trees.

I stopped, and Huck plopped down in the grassy dirt at my feet. I peeked through the trees.

"Our hearts must be full to the brim with fergiveness," said Henry, trying to make his voice sound low and deep. "Our hearts must be overflowin' with generosity fer our neighbor."

Henry stood at the far end of the landing on a big stump and held an open Bible in his hands. Now instead of his too-small suit, he wore a pair of tattered overalls that looked at least a size too big for him. With the pants rolled up and the shoulder straps fixed as short as they could go, he looked like he had as many extra folds and rolls as Huck did.

Then his voice got louder.

"But are we full of fergiveness and generosity?" he bellowed. "*No!*"

A branch snapped as I leaned forward, trying to get a better look at Henry, and he turned around and noticed me holding back a saw palmetto branch, so I could see him. I let go of the branch and walked down the trail toward Uncle Owen's boat which sat on the opposite end of the landing. Henry still stood on his stump pulpit. One of his overall straps had slipped off his shoulder and dangled down his arm like a vine. He didn't look much like a preacher to me, no matter what he tried to make his voice sound like or how much scripture he knew by heart.

"Where ya goin'?" he asked in his regular voice as Huck and I climbed into the boat.

I was thankful Huck was already used to Uncle Owen's boat. It would've been awful embarrassing if Henry would've seen how much trouble I'd had the first time I tried to get Huck into the boat.

"Nowhere," I said.

I sure wasn't about to tell Henry that I was going out in the swamp to search for hog bandit clues so that I could find those bandits and get my picture in the newspaper.

"Isn't that Grandma's Bible?" I asked, changing the subject.

"Yeah," Henry answered. "She borrowed it to me."

"Ya better not git it wet," I warned. "She's awful particular about that Bible. It was her grandma's."

Huck made his way to the front of the boat and found his favorite spot to lie down. Then, he rested his head on the bow, and I grabbed the pole and got ready to shove off.

"How'd ya learn to use Uncle Owen's boat?" Henry asked.

"He taught me," I said. "He says I'm a natural. Probly cuz I've been spendin' my summers in the swamp since I was six."

"Six?" Henry asked, sitting down on his pretend pulpit and letting his feet dangle over the edge of the stump. "Why've ya been comin' here since you was six?"

"Cuz I was born to be a swamper," I said, standing up a bit taller and sticking my chin a bit higher in the air. I held on to the pole like I was born with it in my hand. "I'm gonna live here on Honey Island someday. Plannin' on havin' my own cabin, my own boat, and a whole mess of dogs."

Henry looked at me and shook his head like he felt sorry for me.

"Not me," he said. "I've been called. Just like my daddy was."

"Called?" I asked, resting one end of the pole on the swampy ground near the shore. "By who?"

"God," Henry answered. "To spread the gospel. And while I'm spreadin' it, I'm gonna see the world."

Called by God? I doubted that. I didn't like how Henry was acting all high and mighty about what he was planning to do with his life, making my swamp plans sound so unimportant.

"Well, once ya see the world, y'all know there's no better place than the Okefenokee, so I bet everyplace ya go, you'll wind up wishing ya was right back here," I said, and with that, I pushed hard on the pole, and Huck and I glided out into the waterway leading down toward Billys Lake.

Henry stood up again. I'm sure he was trying to keep his eye on the boat as long as he could because he was just itching to know where we were going. Too bad for him. I'd never tell. I wasn't about to share the glory of saving the swamp from those hog bandits with anyone, especially not Henry James. I only hoped I could figure out a way to find the hog bandits before Uncle Lone did.

Chapter 12

By the time Huck and I got back to Honey Island, Henry wasn't standing on his stump pulpit anymore. Didn't surprise me. Huck and I had been gone for hours. But even so, we hadn't found one single hog bandit clue, and we were worn out.

I jumped up on the landing and dragged the boat into the shrubs so it wouldn't drift away.

"C'mon, Huck," I said, sliding the pole inside the bottom of the boat.

Huck looked at me like he'd rather stay right where he was, but he stood up anyway and loped out of the boat to follow me. As we walked up the trail toward the house, I noticed something blue caught in one of the bushes along the edge of the trail.

Huck sniffed at it, and when I crouched down to get a closer look, I knew exactly what it was. It was the piece of material Grandma used as a bookmark in her Bible. That addlebrained Henry James had let it slip out of the place where it always sat marking Psalm 23, Grandma's favorite passage.

Now who needed forgiveness? I snatched the material from the branch and stomped up toward the yard, hoping I could think of a good way to use this against Henry.

As I pushed open the gate for Huck and me, I looked around. At this time of day, Grandpa was often up on the porch drinking his afternoon jar of tea and rocking in his chair, but the chair was empty. I expected I might see Henry James standing up on the stump near the pecan tree in the yard spouting off more scripture, but the stump was empty too. I wondered where everyone might be.

"C'mon, Huck," I said. "Let's see if anyone's 'round back."

I turned to be sure Huck was following me, and that's when I realized, he wasn't behind me.

I looked past the fence toward the trail but still didn't see him.

"Huck, c'mon!" I yelled.

I went back through the gate so that I could look a little

farther down the trail. I wondered if he had headed back to the boat for another nap. Once I walked back far enough, I saw him sniffing the ground right where we'd found Grandma's bookmark. Then he headed in my direction, keeping his nose to the ground. He sniffed at the dirt like he was looking for something, and he walked in a strange path like he was following an invisible piece of string.

"Whatcha doin', Huck?" I asked, but he acted like he didn't even hear me.

He just kept sniffing and following, sniffing and following. And because he was Huck, he did it all without barking or yipping or growling. So, I followed him. When he got to the yard, he pushed open the gate with his nose, and then he sniffed and walked all around the yard in front of the house and then headed around back. He didn't pay any mind to the chicken yard. I was thankful for that. He meandered past the pump, wound his way around the storage shed, and then headed toward Grandma's garden. That's when I saw Grandma bent over pulling weeds. Henry James sat on a barn stool at the end of the row of snap beans with that Bible lying wide open on his lap. The two of them were so busy talking and laughing with each other that they didn't even see Huck or me coming.

I bet Grandma wouldn't be laughing when I showed her what Huck and I had found on the trail. Huck continued to sniff and meander as he walked that invisible path he followed, while I marched and stomped in a straight line right toward the garden, eager to put a little more fear of Elsie Mae into Henry James. But as we got close to Grandma and Henry, Huck got excited and his sniffing turned almost to dancing. His nose was moving along the dirt like he was chasing crickets or something.

"Why, Elsie Mae, where've ya been?" Grandma asked when she looked up and saw me.

But I didn't even have a chance to answer because the closer Huck got to Grandma and Henry, the more excited he became until his excitement took over completely, and he jumped right up on Henry, knocking him off the stool. Henry went one way. Grandma's Bible went the other. And the pages of scripture fluttered in the air before the book fell with a thud right in the middle of the snap beans Grandma was weeding.

"Sakes alive!" Grandma yelled.

Huck stood over Henry, sniffing and licking him like he was the tastiest bit of food he'd ever smelled or laid eyes on.

"Elsie Mae, come and git this animal offa Henry right now!" Grandma squealed as she hurried over to help Henry.

Animal? Since when did Grandma call Huck an *animal*?

"Huck!" I yelled, slapping my legs.

I rushed over and grabbed the skin on Huck's neck and pulled him off Henry.

"Are ya all right?" Grandma asked as she helped Henry stand up again.

"I think so," Henry said. "But look at yer Bible, Aunt Sarah, I hope Huck didn't ruin it."

Huck? Huck didn't ruin anything. Henry was the one who almost lost Grandma's favorite bookmark.

"Oh my!" Grandma said, looking at her Bible lying there in the dirt and beans.

Henry reached down and picked it up. He brushed off the dirt and straightened out the pages.

"It looks all right," Henry said, handing it to her. "That's a blessing we can all be thankful fer, isn't it?"

"We can also be thankful *this* didn't get lost," I said, holding out Grandma's bookmark toward Henry. "Huck and I found it down by the landin'. *You* must've dropped it when ya were down there playin' preacher."

"Oh, that old thing," Grandma said. "That's just a scrap from one of my old dresses. Not somethin' to worry about, but this Bible's been in my family fer generations," she said, taking it from Henry and holding it to her chest.

I couldn't believe it! Grandma called Huck an animal, *and* she couldn't care less about the special bookmark that I knew had been in her Bible for years saving her favorite passage.

"If that Bible's so important to ya, then ya probably shouldn't let *him* play 'round with it," I said as I nodded toward Henry.

"Oh, nonsense," Grandma said. "Henry James isn't playin' with the Bible. He's preachin' the Word, aren't ya, Henry?"

"Yes, ma'am," Henry said, smiling at me.

I clenched my teeth and knelt next to Huck and rubbed his head, thinking about how I needed to hurry up and find a hog bandit clue so I could be a hero before Henry ruined my entire summer.

Chapter 13

"Well, I been keepin' track of everythin' up here, Pa," Uncle Lone said, tapping the side of his head. "And I think I jus' might be gittin' close to figurin' out what these scoundrels are up to."

The next day, Uncle Owen and Uncle Lone had come by to give Grandma and Grandpa the latest news on the hog bandits. The four of them stood on the front porch talking.

If I was going to solve this mystery, I needed all the information I could get, and I was worried they might leave important things out of the story if they knew I was listening. That's why I hid on the side of the house, peeked around the corner, and listened.

"*Might* be close to figurin' out what they're up to?" Uncle Owen mocked. "Don't take no brains to know what they're doin'. They're takin' the hogs somewhere and sellin' 'em and makin' darn good money. Every swamper family south of Waycross takes such darn good care of their livestock that everybody knows our hogs are the best in the whole state."

"Don't ya think I know that?" Uncle Lone scoffed, taking off his hat and hitting Uncle Owen with it.

"Ya don't know nothin'," Uncle Owen scoffed back, punching Uncle Lone in the arm, "'cept how to be ornery!"

"That's 'nough, y'all!" Grandma scolded, swatting them both with her dishrag.

I held my hand over my mouth to keep my giggles in. Seeing the two of them get in trouble for fighting always made me laugh.

"Zeke, what are we gonna do 'bout this?" Grandma asked.

"These two?" Grandpa answered, pointing to Uncle Lone and Uncle Owen. "Not much we can do 'bout 'em."

I almost laughed out loud. Grandpa did too.

"No!" Grandma said in exasperation. "'Bout those confounded hog bandits. Somethin's gotta be done!"

Just then I heard something behind me, and I turned around to see Henry James standing about two inches from me.

"What're ya doin'?" he asked.

"Shh!" I whispered, putting my fingers to my lips. "None of yer business."

"Yer eavesdroppin', aren't ya?" Henry James asked.

I ignored Henry and turned back around so that I wouldn't miss anything that was happening on the front porch.

"Figurin' out what they're up to isn't the problem," Uncle Owen went on. "It's figurin' out who they are and findin' a way to catch 'em… That's the tricky part."

"The Lord doesn't like eavesdroppin'," Henry said.

I turned back toward Henry.

"It don't say that in the Bible," I said in a loud whisper, almost spitting at Henry.

"How would you know?" he asked.

"Just cuz I don't walk around with the Word of God tucked under my arm like you do doesn't mean I'm a heathen."

"What're ya young'uns squawking about down there?"

I looked up to see Grandpa leaning over the porch railing looking right at Henry and me. Then I looked at Henry, hoping he remembered my toenail digging into the top of his foot, so he'd keep his mouth shut.

"Nothin'," I said. "Any more news on the hog bandits?"

I thought if I got them talking again, maybe they'd forget about asking me why I was peeking around the porch.

"Jus' that they're still out there waitin' fer me to find 'em," Uncle Lone said, sounding as if he really couldn't wait to get his hands on them.

Henry and I walked around to the front of the house and up the porch steps. I sat down on the porch swing, and Henry sat in one of the rocking chairs as Grandpa, Uncle Owen, and Uncle Lone continued their conversation.

"Boys, let's head over to Hamp's," Grandpa said. "Everybody's meetin' up to decide on who's searchin' what part of the swamp when we head out lookin' t'night."

"I ain't goin' to no meetin'," Uncle Lone said, sounding cross. "We're wastin' time. I'm jus' goin' out lookin' fer 'em."

And with that, Uncle Lone walked past Grandpa and down the porch steps, heading for the landing.

"Lone!" Grandma called after him. "There's safety and strength in numbers. Wait till t'night and go in a group."

"Jus' let 'im go, Ma," Uncle Owen said.

"Maybe I could come 'long to the meetin', Uncle Zeke, and lead everyone in a prayer," Henry James offered, leaning forward in the rocking chair and sounding excited at the thought of having a group gathered so that he could practice some public praying.

Grandpa didn't say anything but turned to Grandma with a look that I knew meant he didn't think that was such a good idea. Most swampers were God-fearing folk, but not all of them would take kindly to some ten-year-old boy like Henry James coming around praying over them like he was some high and mighty preacher.

"Henry," Grandma said, "that might not be the best idea at present. Maybe 'nother time."

"Y'all better hurry up. They're waitin' fer ya over at Hamp's," said a voice coming up from the trail.

We all turned to see who it was.

"Millie?" Grandma said.

"Hi, Aunt Millie," I said.

Though Millie wasn't a blood relative, I had been calling her "aunt" since my first summer in the swamp.

"What're ya doin' here?" Grandma asked.

"We're hemmin' my dress t'day," Aunt Millie said, walking through the gate, across the yard, and up the porch steps. "Don't ya r'member? Fer the frolic?"

"I completely fergot," Grandma said. "With all this hog bandit nonsense goin' on, it's a wonder I r'member anythin' anymore."

"Well, when I left Ed over at Hamp's, I heard everyone talkin' 'bout somethin' no one's likely to fergit any time soon," Aunt Millie said.

"What's that?" Grandma asked.

"That it's a mite strange that the only family not to lose a hog yet is yers," Aunt Millie said.

The snippy tone of her voice reminded me of the way my sisters sometimes talked to me when Mama wasn't home, so I knew Aunt Millie didn't just *hear* everyone talking about this over at Hamp's. She *believed* whatever folks were saying about it.

"What is *that* supposed to mean?" Grandma asked, sounding like she wanted to do more than just hem Aunt Millie's dress.

"Well, ya know," Aunt Millie stammered. "Jus' what folks is wonderin' is all."

Now she sounded like she was backpedaling some, just like my sisters usually did once they realized I could tell Mama on them.

But then she mustered up a little courage somehow because she went on and made her point. "Ya gotta admit it's a li'l suspicious is all. 'Specially with the sorted past one of yer boys has had."

"Nothin' suspicious 'bout it," Grandpa said.

"'Cept if they're all accusin' us a somethin'," Uncle Lone spat out.

We all turned to see Uncle Lone standing on the other side of the front fence. He must've seen Aunt Millie comin' up the trail and still been close enough to hear what she was saying. Aunt Millie looked about as scared as a hog must look when one of the hog bandits showed up in the hog pen.

"Accusin' *me*, that is!" Uncle Lone said, sounding worse than ornery as he pushed the front gate open a little too hard, stormed across the yard, and headed straight up the porch steps toward Aunt Millie.

She might've started squealing like a hog being hog-napped by a hog bandit, if it weren't for Uncle Owen stepping in between the two of them.

"Take it easy, Lone," Uncle Owen said. "Let's jus' head over to Hamp's. No one, hogs or otherwise, is gonna rest easy till we find them bandits."

Uncle Lone peered around Uncle Owen to glare at Aunt Millie while she shuffled her feet nervously, making hollow sounds on the wooden porch.

"Owen's right," Grandpa said. "C'mon, boys, we'll take my boat. Let's go."

"I tol' ya. I ain't goin'." Uncle Lone snorted, still shooting daggers at Aunt Millie with his stare. "I ain't 'bout to go help a bunch a folks who's actin' as if *I'm* suspect."

"They ain't sayin' that," Uncle Owen said, knowing that if he wanted to keep peace, he'd have to settle Uncle Lone down some. "Let's jus' go."

"Who needs 'em," Uncle Lone said, stomping down the porch steps. "I'm gonna be the one to catch those hog bandits once and fer all, and I'll do it on my own. Then we'll see what everyone says 'bout this family."

And as he took off across the yard, through the gate, and down the trail, Grandma called, "Lone! C'mon now!"

Aunt Millie let out a sigh of relief.

"Let 'im go," Grandpa said. "He'll come 'round. C'mon, Owen. Let's git movin'."

So Grandpa and Uncle Owen headed down the porch steps too.

I jumped up from the swing and called after them, "Uncle Owen, since yer boat's here and yer goin' with Grandpa, can I use it again t'day?"

"Sure," Uncle Owen called over his shoulder.

Grandma opened the screen door to let Aunt Millie inside, and I heard her whisper in a voice she didn't think was loud enough for me to hear, "Millie Gibson, y'all better git on in here, and if ya know what's good for ya, ya won't make any more mention 'bout those hog bandits, or I might jus' use my thread to sew that sharp tongue of yers inside yer mouth fer good."

I could tell by the look on Henry James's face that he'd heard it too, and I wasn't sure who looked more surprised, Aunt Millie or Henry. But I knew Grandma didn't care. She gave Uncle Lone what's for all the time, but that didn't mean anyone else could go around saying things about him. And I knew she'd never apologize to anyone for that, no matter how surprised they were to find out that her tongue was sharper than her sewing scissors.

Chapter 14

"C'mon, Huck," I said, heading down the porch steps. "Let's go."

"Where ya goin'?" Henry stood up and called after me.

"Nowhere," I yelled, not looking back.

"Can I come?"

I kept going, pretending not to hear, but outside the gate, Huck found something on the ground. It was a green handkerchief. He sniffed at it and pranced around it, getting all excited. The handkerchief was the same color as Aunt Millie's dress. She'd probably dropped it on her way up the trail. I didn't want to go back to give it to her because that would just give Henry James another chance to pester me about taking him along.

"We'll git it later, boy," I said. "C'mon."

I kept walking, but Huck didn't follow. Instead, he sniffed some more and began heading in the opposite direction back up toward the house. He sniffed the ground and walked like he was following that invisible thread again, just like he had done the day before with Grandma's bookmark. I didn't want to, but I turned and picked up the handkerchief and followed Huck back into the yard. As I did, I watched him walk in the exact same path Aunt Millie had.

Henry was sitting in the rocking chair again, this time pushing his feet against the porch floor, moving himself back and forth. When he saw Huck and me coming back, he stopped the chair and wiped his hands across his face. Had he been crying? What did he have to cry about? But then I remembered why Henry James was here. I was so busy being mad at him for ruining my summer that I had almost forgotten that his mama and daddy had just dumped him here without even telling him when they'd be back. That had to be crummy!

I felt a twinge in my stomach. The same kind of twinge I felt last year when I let one of the boys at school get in trouble for tying the girls' jump rope in knots when *I* had been the one to do it. I just thought it would be funny to see all those prissy girls crying because they couldn't twirl and jump and sing their stupid, silly songs, but it wasn't all that funny when

I heard that Harry Hickox got in trouble from his daddy for having to stay after school all week.

I sighed.

But I pushed back at that feeling in my stomach. It wasn't *my* fault that Henry had been left at Honey Island for the summer. It wasn't *my* fault that his mama and daddy were more worried about saving other people's souls than taking care of their own son. And what was I supposed to do about it anyway? And just when I felt that twinge in my stomach sinking away, I noticed the hopeful look on Henry's face. The one that told me he hoped I had changed my mind about taking him with me, and that bad feeling in my stomach bobbed to the surface again.

So, I looked away from Henry and kept watching Huck until he finally followed the invisible path up the porch steps. He stopped at the screen door and scratched at the porch floor right outside the door.

I let him scratch a bit until finally Grandma yelled, "Elsie Mae, come git that dog of yers!"

She didn't know I was standing right there watching Huck try to dig a hole in the porch floor. Henry James watched too, but neither of us did anything, and Huck kept scratching.

"*Elsie Mae!*" Grandma yelled again.

I looked at Henry, and then I did something I knew I shouldn't do, but just had to. I had to see if Huck would do the same thing to Aunt Millie that he had done to Henry James, so I reached for the handle on the screen door and opened it, letting Huck inside. I knew what he'd most likely do, and I knew Grandma would be beyond addled when he did it. Even more, I knew Aunt Millie would be outraged, but I had to see if what I thought was going to happen really did happen.

Once inside the house, Huck kept following the invisible line that I knew would lead right to his prize—Aunt Millie.

"Elsie Mae," Grandma said through the pins she held between her teeth. "What're ya lettin' Huck in here fer?"

I didn't answer Grandma, but only stood silently in the doorway watching Huck get more and more excited with every sniff until he was right up next to Aunt Millie. And that's when it happened. He jumped right up on top of her, knocking her clear off the bench she sat on.

"*Help!*" Millie screamed. "*Help!*"

Huck sniffed her. Huck slobbered on her. Huck attacked her like she was one of Grandma's huckleberry pies. All while Millie squealed like a hog.

"Elsie Mae, git on over here and git this *animal* offa her," Grandma wailed, spitting out the pins she held in her mouth and tossing Aunt Millie's dress onto the table so she could help her.

"He's killin' me! He's killin' me!" Millie whined, fighting off Huck's slobbery tongue.

I let go of the screen door that I was still holding and ran in after Huck. I grabbed the extra skin around his neck that I now almost thought of as a handle and pulled him across the floor toward the door.

"What in tarnation made ya let that beast in here, child?" Aunt Millie exclaimed as she sat up on the floor.

"I'm sorry," I said.

"Elsie Mae," Grandma said, reaching down to help Aunt Millie to her feet, "git that dog outta here, and ya better find a way to keep 'im from scarin' people half to death or we're gonna have to git rid of 'im."

"Yes, ma'am," I said, pulling Huck out on the porch again. "We won't bother ya again. We're goin' out in Uncle Owen's boat anyway."

Henry James, who had been watching the whole scene unfold, used my misery as his opportunity.

"Aunt Sarah?" he called through the screen. "Is it all right if I go out in the boat with Elsie Mae and Huck?"

I glared at him, but he knew he had weaseled his way

into coming along. He knew Grandma would say yes, and he knew if she did, I couldn't say no, especially after what had just happened with Aunt Millie.

"That'd be jus' fine," Grandma said. "Might be best if y'all stick together from now on. What with the hog bandits runnin' 'round and that dog of Elsie's actin' all wild lately."

"Thanks!" Henry called as he jumped off the porch without even using the steps.

Oh great! Now Grandma thought Henry and I should stick together. That meant I was probably not just stuck with Henry for the afternoon. I was probably stuck with him for the rest of the summer, or at least until we found those hog bandits, which was what I intended to do.

But now, not only did I have to figure out how to find the hog bandits before Uncle Lone or anyone else did, I had to do it with Henry James and his hallelujahs tagging along with me everywhere I went.

Chapter 15

"Don't stand up," I said. "Because if ya fall in, I'm not gonna save ya. 'Sides, if ya fall in, the gators'll probly eat ya 'fore I even have time to think 'bout savin' ya."

I pushed hard against the landing, and Uncle Owen's boat floated out into the waterway leading away from Honey Island. I stood in the center of the boat. Huck lay in the front as if he were the captain of a ship. Our lowly second-class passenger, Henry, sat all the way in the back.

"How many gators are out there d'ya think?" Henry asked, sounding scared.

"How many?" I laughed. "How many? Uncle Owen said some parts of the swamp got so many that at night when they come out, their heads all lay next to each other and ya can walk on 'em like ya was Peter walkin' on the water. There's one right now," I said, pointing to a log along the edge of the waterway where a five-foot gator lay sunning himself.

I didn't mention to Henry that Uncle Owen had told me that's how many gators there *used* to be in the swamp. There weren't nearly that many anymore. Too many folks came around hunting nowadays. But even so, there were still a lot of gators out there, and maybe I was actually doing right by keeping Henry a little afraid. He'd be safer that way. And he never had to know that out of all the creatures in the swamp, it was the gators that scared me the most.

"Hey, I've got an idea," I said. "Want me to show ya Hollow Log Pond?"

"OK," Henry said. "I guess."

I decided I'd make Henry James sorry that he'd found a way to tag along with me, and a visit to Hollow Log Pond might be just the trick.

Hollow Log Pond got its name because even in the daylight it was so dark that it felt like being inside a hollow log. But worse than the darkness of it were the edges of the pond that were so mushy and mucky you could get swallowed up. It was the kind of place even the swampers stayed away from. But I didn't care. Even though the gators in the swamp scared me some, a dark, spooky pond didn't scare me much at all.

As we got closer to the pond, I turned around to see if Henry was getting scared yet, and the look in his eyes told me he was. I turned back around and smiled to myself while I pushed hard on the pole as the boat continued to glide deeper and deeper into the swamp.

"Some folks think Hollow Log Pond is haunted by the spirits of the Seminoles who died here in the Okefenokee," I said.

"Seminoles?" Henry asked.

"Yeah, Indians," I said. "People say they was hidin' out here when they was runnin' away from some of the first swamp settlers. Some folks say they got swallowed up in the swampy ground, and that's why ya can sometimes still hear 'em callin' out."

"Really?" Henry said, sounding like he might be thinking he should've stayed back in the safety of that rocking chair on the porch.

I wasn't lying to Henry. Folks did tell stories like these, and lots of Indians did die in the swamp, but I was stretching the truth a bit by saying their voices could be heard coming up through the swampy ground.

"How much farther is it?" Henry asked as the thick trees and bushes closed in around us and the waterway we glided through got even more narrow, making it feel like dusk even though it was daytime.

"Just a li'l ways more," I answered.

That's when I heard Henry whisper, "'The Lord is my shepherd. I shall not want…'"

I recognized those words. Grandma's favorite passage where her bookmark always rested: Psalm 23. Henry wasn't standing on his stump pulpit being so high and mighty anymore. He was praying as if to save his life. I sighed with satisfaction. His desperate pleas for protection were an answer to *my* prayers.

The boat finally reached Hollow Log Pond. It wasn't much more than an oversize puddle surrounded by a thick layer of bushes and trees—a forest-like fortress wall that not only cut out almost all the light from the bright noontime sun but also protected the pond from the scorching summer heat. Only a few faint swamp sounds—a faraway bird calling or a distant breeze bending the tops of the cypress branches—broke through the silence of the pond's seclusion that surrounded us.

"This is it?" Henry said, his voice sounding ghostlike as it echoed off the smooth surface of the dark tea-colored water.

"Can't ya feel it?" I asked, trying to make Henry even more scared than he looked.

"What?" he whispered.

"That cold, damp feelin'," I answered.

"Yeah," Henry answered. "What 'bout it?"

"That's the Seminoles' spirits," I said. "Tryin' to escape their doom."

Now I wasn't just stretching the truth. I was telling a story. A story that was a lie, but I just needed to be sure that Henry wouldn't beg to tag along with me everywhere I went from now on.

Henry rubbed his hands on his arms as if he were trying to keep the spirits from touching his skin.

"'The Lord is my shepherd...'" Henry started again, only this time he wasn't whispering. He was speaking out loud. Probably hoping to scare those spirits away with scripture.

"Yer not scared, are ya?" I asked, laughing a little.

But Henry didn't have time to answer because just then there was a huge rustling in the trees on the right side of the pond. Huck, who had been sleeping, lifted his head.

I had been standing since we'd left Honey Island, but I sat down and looked at Henry.

"What was that?" I asked in a loud whisper.

Most times something rustling in the woods meant an animal was nearby, but it didn't sound like an animal to me. I felt myself getting as scared as Henry looked.

Henry rocked back and forth.

"'Fear not fer I am with you, says the Lord,'" he whispered closing his eyes.

I thought back to Huck stealing those eggs, me trying to get Henry in trouble with Grandma's bookmark, the eaves-dropping on the porch, and me bringing Henry out here to Hollow Log Pond to scare him. Maybe Henry was right. My sins were finding me out right now.

Was God bringing up the Seminole spirits for real to teach *me* a lesson? Or maybe even scare me to death?

I sat silently looking over toward where the sound had come from, but I didn't see anything in the thick, damp darkness. I looked all around the pond for anything that could've made that sound. Maybe it was just a squirrel or a possum, but it sounded like something much larger than that. Could it be a bear?

Then I heard whispering. The hairs on the back of my neck prickled, and Huck stood up.

"Who would be out here?" I whispered to Henry, who still had his eyes closed.

With wide eyes, I kept searching the wall of darkness that surrounded us, but I still didn't see anything.

"*Who's there?*" a deep voice called through the trees.

My heart pounded, and I don't know if it was so loud that it made Henry open his eyes, but he did.

"*Y'all better answer!*" warned a second voice even meaner sounding than the first one.

Henry looked right at me, and our eyes locked in fear.

Huck scratched at the wooden seat he stood on, and I knew if that lumpy scar on his neck wasn't there, he'd be whimpering and growling and barking for sure.

Without making a sound, I mouthed to Henry, "I wonder if it's the hog bandits?"

And then, *Crack!*

A gun went off.

I grabbed the pole, stood up, and pushed into the mucky, mushy ground on the edge of Hollow Log Pond harder than I've ever pushed before. Henry closed his eyes again. He folded his hands. And he rocked back and forth while his lips prayed silent prayers. Huck shifted around and got so agitated that I worried he might jump out of the boat. And as I pushed and dug at the swampy ground, weaving us out of the pond and back up the waterway toward Billys Lake, I hoped that Henry James really had been called by God and that God was listening right now as Henry James called back to him.

Chapter 16

"Grandpa! Grandpa!" I yelled, running up the trail toward the house. I slammed through the front gate, and when I didn't see him in the front yard or up on the porch, I ran around back toward the barn.

I sure hoped he was back from Hamp's by now.

When I got to the backyard, Grandpa stood next to the barn, raking through some dried brush. He looked up when he saw me.

I was almost out of breath but managed to have just enough left to say, "Somebody jus' shot at us!"

Huck and Henry James came running up behind me panting.

Grandpa leaned on his rake and asked, "What in tarnation 'r' you talkin' 'bout, Elsie Mae?"

"Jus' now, we was out in Hollow Log Pond, and we heard somethin' in the bushes, and at first I thought it might be an animal, and I looked 'round but couldn't see nothin', and turns out there was two men hidin' in the woods. They was whisperin', and then they yelled, and then we heard a gun go off."

"A gun?" Grandpa asked. "Are ya sure 'bout that?"

Grandpa didn't seem nearly as concerned as I thought he should be. Didn't he believe me?

"What'd they look like?" Grandpa asked as he began pulling the rake through the brush again.

"Well, we didn't actually see 'em," I said, looking over at Henry. "Ya know how dark Hollow Log Pond is, Grandpa."

"That I do," Grandpa said. "It's black as pitch in there. Likely they was some fools down from Waycross comin' to hunt. Folks do it all the time. Fact last month a coupla fellows got themselves stuck in the muck in there, and the sheriff had to come git 'em out.

"So more'n likely it was somebody that don't know no better who got themselves lost and ended up in that good-fer-nothin' pond. Y'all and that dog of yers probably scared 'em half to death."

Henry James stepped forward and spoke up. "Scared

107

them half to death? I don't think so, sir. I ain't mean no disrespect, Uncle Zeke, but I was so scared I think I almost caught a glimpse of Glory."

Grandpa chuckled.

"Grandpa, I don't think it's nothin' to laugh 'bout," I said. "I think they wanted to scare us cuz they're up to somethin' no good. I could jus' feel it."

I felt Huck sitting at my side, and I reached down and scratched him on the head without even taking my eyes off Grandpa, hoping Grandpa'd somehow realize the importance of what had just happened.

"Yeah, Uncle Zeke," Henry James spoke up again, "I know yer not supposed to, but I'd swear on a stack of Holy Bibles that those fellas were trouble."

"Ya think they might could be the hog bandits?" I asked.

"I doubt that," Grandpa said. "Wouldn't make much sense fer the hog bandits t'be over in Hollow Log Pond in the middle of the day shootin' at a coupla a young'uns and a dog. Even so," Grandpa said, nodding his head toward us, "y'all better stay away from that pond then because ya don't need no more trouble. Huck's gittin' into 'nough trouble fer all three of ya."

"Oh no!" I said. "What'd he do now?"

"Well, 'sides the fact that I heard he like to almost kilt yer aunt Millie earlier t'day, yer grandma found the laundry that she hung up behind the barn early this mornin' scattered all over the yard."

I wondered when Huck had had the chance to do that.

"Is Grandma mad 'bout it?" I asked.

"Well, she ain't too happy 'bout her favorite dress that's got holes in it that no doubt match Huck's teeth."

I gave Huck a sideways look—the kind of look that Mama gave me when I came home late for supper or forgot to do one of my chores.

"Don't fret too much though," Grandpa said. "Ya know yer grandma. She'll git over it, but I'd keep a better eye on Huck if I was you, or she might jus' make ya keep 'im tied up."

Tied up? I couldn't let that happen. Huck needed his freedom just like I did. I'd have to be sure he didn't get into any more trouble.

"I reckon it's jus' 'bout time to eat," Grandpa said, getting back to work. "Why don't ya young'uns go on and find yerself somethin' t'do till then?"

Huck, Henry James, and I headed back around toward the front of the house.

"And stay away from Hollow Log Pond," Grandpa

called after us. "If yer grandma hears y'all got people shootin' at ya, she'll keep ya on a shorter leash than the one she wants to put on Huck."

Chapter 17

"We better listen to Uncle Zeke," Henry James said the next day after breakfast.

"But how can we?" I asked. "If those men really are the hog bandits, shouldn't we find 'em so the hogs'll be safe?"

Huck, Henry James, and I sat out in Uncle Owen's boat in the middle of Billys Lake. The sun barely peeked over the tall cypress trees, and the morning breeze still felt a tiny bit cool. My stomach hurt from eating one too many of Grandma's biscuits at breakfast.

"We don't even know fer sure that it really *was* the hog bandits yesterday," Henry said.

"Well, we don't know it wasn't," I said. "'Sides, who else could it be?"

Before yesterday, I had no intention of including

Henry James in my search for the hog bandits, but after what happened at Hollow Log Pond, I thought maybe Henry and his hallelujahs might not be such a bad thing to have around.

"Ya know what the Lord says?" Henry James asked. "'Vengeance is mine.' So let's jus' leave the hog bandits to the Lord."

"Oh, vengeance smengence," I said. "I want to stop those hog bandits, and I'll do it myself if I have to. Well, me and Huck, that is."

I was talking tough, but I knew I needed Henry *and* his prayers in order to face the dangers lurking in Hollow Log Pond, even if it meant sharing some of the glory if and when we did find those hog bandits.

"What if we jus' go back to the pond," I continued, "and after we make sure no one's around, we look to see if there're any clues about who those two low-downs were who was shootin' at us jus' to see if they *might* be the hog bandits."

The sun was inching its way higher in the sky, and Henry squinted at me.

"I don't know, Elsie Mae," he said. "Sounds dangerous to me. 'Sides, Uncle Zeke told us not to go back to Hollow Log Pond."

"But if we find the hog bandits, or even jus' *help* find

them, Grandpa Zeke'll be so happy he'll forget all 'bout what he tol' us," I said. "C'mon, Henry."

Henry sat with his lips pressed together. I knew there was so much scripture floating around in that head of his, I doubted that he'd be able to find the courage to go against all of it and listen to me.

"I'll let ya practice one of yer sermons on me," I said, trying to bargain with him.

Henry still didn't say anything.

"How 'bout two?" I asked, sweetening the deal. "I'll listen to two whole sermons."

Still nothing.

"OK, I'll let you practice one sermon a day on me, every day, for the rest of the summer, and I'll make Huck listen too."

Looking thoughtful, Henry scratched his head while I crossed my fingers, hoping he was getting close to saying yes.

"I have a better idea," he said. "But if ya don't agree to it, I'm not goin' back to Hollow Log Pond with ya. Ever."

Chapter 18

That afternoon, I had another stomachache, but this time it wasn't from eating too many of Grandma's biscuits. In fact, I hadn't been able to eat much dinner at all. Now my stomach hurt because I had agreed to let Henry James "practice" baptize me in Billys Lake. It was the only way he'd agree to go back to Hollow Log Pond with me.

Henry sat in the back of the boat with Grandma's Bible resting on his lap and a big grin covering his face.

After finishing dinner with Grandma, Grandpa, Uncle Owen, and Uncle Lone, we were lucky that they all had a mess of work to do. Grandma and Grandpa went around back to work in the garden and the barn, and Uncle Owen and Uncle Lone headed over to their place to fix their fence that needed a new gate.

Henry and I were both smart enough to know that if any of them had any idea what the two of us were up to, not only would Grandma not want her Bible anywhere near Billys Lake, but none of them would ever agree to Henry and me getting out of the boat and into the water without one of them nearby to watch over us. So, we had sneaked Grandma's Bible out of the house without telling anyone where we were going or what we were planning to do.

I poled the boat along much more slowly than usual. I wasn't in any hurry to get there. It wasn't the baptism part that worried me. It was the gators. Even Uncle Owen had been scared of the gators when he and Daddy were baptized all those years ago. And there wasn't much that scared the two of them. Now I was heading out into the swamp to do the same thing, and even though I knew there weren't as many gators in the swamp as there used to be, I also knew there were plenty enough that might like to take a bite out of Henry and me.

I turned around and looked at Henry. Even though we'd almost made it through the waterway leading away from Honey Island, which meant we'd be at the lake soon, Henry looked as happy as Huck had looked the day he ate Grandma's huckleberry pie. Maybe when you've got God on your side and you're doing his work, he gives you special courage or something. God sure hadn't blessed me with any of that courage because the closer we got to the spot we'd picked out for the baptism, the more I kept thinking about changing my mind. But doing the practice baptism was the only way Henry James would agree to go back to Hollow Log Pond with me.

"Henry," I said, turning around, "do ya really think this is a good idea?"

"It's not jus' a good idea," Henry answered. "This might could be why I was sent to the Okefenokee this summer—to baptize ya!"

"Well, it's just a practice baptism, Henry," I said. "It's not a real one. Yer not even a real preacher."

"The Lord works in mysterious ways, Elsie Mae," Henry said. "And we don't always know and understand 'em."

"Well, I jus' hope his mysterious ways don't include us bein' a meal for the gators," I said, hoping to scare him, even though I didn't have much hope left for that.

Once Henry got his heart set on baptizing me, I'd tried to discourage him with all the gator stories Uncle Owen had told me over the years, but Henry had a scripture passage for every tale I told—*"The Lord protects the righteous." "Those the Lord calls he protects." "The Lord will put his hedge of protection around his children."*

"The only thing left fer us t'do," Henry said, "is to trust and obey."

I really found it hard to believe that the two of us getting out of the boat in Billys Lake was something God wanted us to do. Weren't we supposed to use the good sense he gave us? That's what Mama always said when I did something she thought was foolish. I didn't even have to wonder what she'd think of this.

By the time we reached the place on the other side of the lake that I knew was about waist deep, I didn't just have a stomachache, but now my head hurt too. Probably because I'd been squinting against the sun the whole way, searching the surface for gators in the water.

Uncle Owen and I had fished in this spot lots of times last summer, and I remember how it was shallow enough to see the bottom. But at the same time, I knew it was deep enough for Henry to dunk me.

Last summer, when there hadn't been all kinds of hog bandit ruckus going on, Uncle Owen and I had had lots of time to do fun things like fish and take long boat rides together, but this year was turning out different in so many ways.

Once the boat slid close enough to the swamp's edge so that it rested on the muddy bottom of the shallow water, I sat down on the middle seat and slid the paddle inside the bottom of the boat.

"Ready?" Henry asked.

"Well, aren't ya gonna give some kinda sermon or somethin' first?" I asked.

I wasn't in the habit of encouraging Henry to practice his preaching, but I just wasn't quite ready to get into the water yet.

"I was goin' t'do it once we got in the water," Henry said.

"Oh no," I said. "Yer gonna give the message while we're sittin' in the safety of this here boat. Then when yer ready t'do the dunkin' part, that's when we'll git in."

"OK," Henry said, opening the Bible and standing up.

The boat rocked, and I looked at him.

"Jus' cuz we're out here for the baptism, if ya fall in, I ain't jumpin' in to rescue ya," I said.

My voice sounded angry, but my insides felt scared. I was so at home here in the Okefenokee, no matter what part of the swamp I was in, but getting out of the boat was a whole different story, especially if I wasn't with Uncle Owen or Grandpa.

"I'm not gonna fall in," Henry James said. "Stop worryin'. I'm out here answerin' God's call, and he's got his angels 'round me right now. 'Round you too, Elsie Mae. You'll see."

"Well, I hope those angels got a coupla pistols so if any gators git near us, they can shoot 'em in the head," I said, scanning the water for bumpy gator backs breaking the surface.

"Angels got more power than pistols, Elsie Mae," Henry said, sounding as if I'd just said the most foolish thing a person could say.

I couldn't understand how come Henry wasn't more afraid. After the way he'd acted in Hollow Log Pond the other day and the way he was so scared to go back there, I couldn't believe he was so brave about getting out of the boat and into the water. Maybe he really *did* hear God calling him to be a preacher and that's what was giving him courage. But after what I'd overheard Grandpa say about Henry's daddy, I kind of doubted the whole call-from-God thing.

The other evening after I went to bed, Grandma and Grandpa thought I was asleep, and I overheard them talking.

"Well, it shouldn't surprise ya that Henry wants to be a preacher, Sarah. That daddy of his could persuade a fish to buy a boat. He convinced yer sister to marry 'im only a few weeks after gittin' outta Folkston. And, even 'fore he met her, look how much trouble he got Lone into."

"Oh, jus' hush up, would ya, Zeke," Grandma scolded. "I don't want the kids to hear ya jibber-jabbering like that."

"I ain't jibber-jabberin', Sarah," Grandpa said matter-a-factly. "I'm speakin' the truth. And ya know it. Henry's daddy is the king of connivers."

"Hush!" Grandma said, putting an end to their conversation once and for all.

After that, they were quiet for a few minutes and then started talking about something else. But I'd heard enough to make me wonder about Henry. Maybe he *was* just like his daddy, persuading people to do what *he* wanted.

"Jus' hurry up and preach, would ya?" I said, swatting at a black fly buzzing around my head. "I want to git this over with."

"Elsie Mae," Henry said, sounding like he was trying to act older than I was, even though *he* was a whole year younger than me. "The Spirit cannot be rushed, and patience is a virtue."

I sighed and folded my arms over my chest.

"Let's begin with a verse that proves beyond a shadow of a doubt that God loves us all," Henry said, flipping the pages of Grandma's Bible to find the verse he was looking for.

Then he read John 3:16, which I had memorized in

Sunday school way back in first grade. I sighed again, but this time louder.

When he finished reading, Henry said, "Now, knowing that God loves us is only part of the gospel message."

He continued, trying to make his voice sound deep and important. "We must first know that we need God. 'Fer the wages of sin is death, but the gift of God is eternal life…'"

Henry's voice echoed out over the calm, glass-like water. The sun hung in the open blue sky over Billys Lake, and I got hotter and hotter as I stared up at Henry.

"Yes, that's right! We are *all* sinners! We *all* need fergiveness! And we *all* need to be saved!"

The way he said *all* so many times, I wondered if he meant Huck too. I looked over at Huck sleeping in the front of the boat. After these last few days, Huck had been an even bigger sinner than I had, and that was saying a lot.

"Now let's sing one verse of 'Jesus Paid It All,'" Henry said.

He began singing, and I joined him. I had sung this hymn at church so many times that I not only knew the first verse by heart, but all four verses. Near the end of the chorus, I thought about acting as if I was so overcome with the Spirit that I couldn't help myself from continuing with verses two, three, and four just to buy myself a little more time in the boat, but I decided I'd better just stop singing and get this whole thing over with.

"All right," Henry said. "It's time."

He laid Grandma's Bible on the seat behind him, held on to the sides of the boat, and stepped over the side into the ankle-deep water. I stood up, held on to the boat just like he did, scanned the water's surface and the swamp's edge for gators, and stepped into the water with Henry. My feet sank some and disappeared in the murky bottom.

"OK," Henry said. "We'll need to be in water that's about waist deep so I'll be able to dunk ya."

We both shuffled our feet through the muck we were standing in to get to deeper water, and with every inch deeper we went, the ground squished more, as if each step brought us closer to getting swallowed up.

Uncle Owen had told me stories about folks practically getting buried alive in the muck and murk of the Okefenokee. It was stories like these that made the Indians, who had lived here before the swampers, give the swamp the name Okefenokee, which meant "Land of the Trembling Earth." Right now, I knew I was feeling exactly what those first Indians had felt when they gave the swamp its name. The only difference was that I thought *I* was trembling even more than the earth beneath me.

"This is far enough," I said once the water reached the top of my thighs.

Surprisingly, Henry didn't argue with me. Maybe his answering-God's-call courage was trembling a little too. He looked back at the boat, which rested up along the swamp's edge in the shallow water, and I wondered if maybe he was going to chicken out before he even did the baptism.

"I wanted to read somethin' from Isaiah," Henry said. "But I fergot the Bible in the boat."

"Fergit it, Henry," I said. "Jus' pray or make somethin' up. We're not goin' back to the boat and comin' all the way back out here."

"But I had the perfect passage picked out for this," Henry whined.

"If we go back to the boat, Henry, I'm *not* comin' back out here," I said.

"OK, OK," Henry said, sounding flustered.

"Why don't we jus' say John 3:16 together?" I suggested, wanting to get on with it.

"Ya know John 3:16?" Henry asked. "How do ya know that?"

"I told ya before," I said. "Jus' because I don't walk 'round with a Bible all day doesn't mean I'm a worse sinner than you."

Henry gave me an annoyed look.

"I learned it in Sunday school," I said. "Now, c'mon. Let's jus' say the verse, and then ya can dunk me."

We said the verse together as if we were reciting it in front of our Sunday school teacher in hopes of getting a gold star on the attendance chart. But even though I'd said and heard those words many times before, as I looked around while we said them, the hugeness of the sky, the tallness of the trees, and the shininess of the water all somehow felt a little different.

"Elsie Mae, d'you believe?" Henry asked in a big preacher voice.

And I heard myself say, a little louder than I expected, "I believe!"

"I baptize ya in the name of the Father, Son, and Spirit."

Next thing I knew, Henry James held one of my arms across my chest while he put the other hand on my back. Then he leaned me back into the water, dunking me all the way under like he'd been baptizing people his whole life. And before I knew what happened, he pushed me forward, popping me back out of the water again, and I came up sputtering.

"Hallelujah, Elsie, I did it!" Henry shrieked. "I did it! I baptized ya!"

I smiled at him as the water dripped down my face and said, "You'll probly end up bein' a better preacher than yer daddy."

And Henry smiled back at me. But, even though I *did* somehow feel different and *was* truly excited for Henry, I still had gators on my mind.

"C'mon, Henry," I said. "Let's git back to the boat."

So, we both shuffled our way back through the murky muck toward the boat.

"Looks like our witness slept through the whole thing," I said, pointing to Huck lying in the bow of the boat.

We both laughed, which was probably why Henry didn't see where he was stepping. And in an instant, his laughter turned into a terrified scream.

I screamed too as Henry raced forward in a flying leap. He grabbed the side of the boat, rocking it hard. Huck woke up with a start. He slid and scratched. His claws dug into the wooden seat.

As Huck tried to right himself, the boat rocked harder and higher. I watched Grandma's Bible slide from side to side across the wooden seat in the back of the boat. Henry scrambled up into the shrubs at the swamp's edge, doing anything he could to get out of the water.

"Henry! What's wrong?" I yelled.

Had a gator sent Henry scurrying out of the swamp? I couldn't wait for an answer.

I plunged toward the boat, hoping I wasn't about to step into a wide-open mouth full of sharp teeth.

I also hoped that if my newly baptized soul wasn't on its way to heaven, I could by some miracle get to the boat before Huck rocked it so hard that Grandma's Bible went overboard.

When I was almost close enough to touch the boat, my foot landed on something hard. Something round! Something bumpy! What was it?

A turtle!

A huge turtle!

Henry had stepped on a turtle!

I sighed with relief as I stumbled forward, almost falling face-first in the shallow water. I somehow managed to stay on my feet, but just as soon as I felt certain my soul would be granted more time on this earth, Huck's scratching and clawing and rocking sent Grandma's Bible sliding off the seat toward the bottom of the boat.

I lunged over the side, hoping to save the Bible from

falling into the dirty water that lay at the bottom of the boat. But as I reached out to grab it, the pages fluttered through my fingertips as it fell toward the puddle.

I ended up with the Bible in one hand and a single, jagged-edged ripped page in the other.

Chapter 19

O f all the pages, why did it have to be Psalm 23?" I asked. "If it was a page from Haggai or Malachi, she'd probably never miss it. No one ever reads those books of the Bible."

"It's a punishment," Henry James said solemnly. "Fer our sins."

"I thought ya was out there talkin' 'bout fergiveness this mornin', not punishment," I said as I pushed the pole guiding the boat between the trees of the narrow waterway we traveled.

Thankfully, when we'd gotten back from the baptism, Grandma and Grandpa had still been busy working out back, so it was easy as huckleberry pie to sneak her Bible back to the place where she kept it by her bed. We'd made sure to stick the Psalm 23 page next to the bookmark right where it belonged.

Then I'd sneaked as many leftover biscuits as I could

carry and a jar of honey out to the front yard so that we could have a snack in the sun while our clothes dried. Once I'd made it through the baptism without a gator making a meal out of me, my nervous stomach wasn't nervous anymore. It was just plain hungry.

But even with the Bible safely back in place, guilt had overcome Henry the way Huck had pounced on him that day in the garden. And it wouldn't let him go. Now *he* had the nervous stomach, but I didn't care. That had left all the biscuits for Huck and me, and while I'd finished licking all the honey from my fingers, I'd begged Henry to go back out in the boat with me. Finally, he'd given in.

Once I had him out in the boat, I'd somehow persuaded him that going back to Hollow Log Pond was somehow the right thing to do.

So now we were finally on our way.

"We shoulda never taken Aunt Sarah's Bible without her permission," Henry said. "And we shouldn't be goin' back to Hollow Log Pond either when Uncle Zeke tol' us not to go."

"But we made a deal," I said for about the hundredth time. "I kept up my part, and if ya don't keep up yer part, that's a sin jus' the same as disobeyin' yer elders."

I knew my logic wasn't exactly scriptural, but I didn't

care. I had risked my life out in Billys Lake getting baptized, and now I really had my heart set on finding those hog bandits or at least some kind of clue. And I needed Henry to go with me. He had made a promise.

"'Sides," I added, "we find those hog bandits and all will be fergiven."

Henry sighed.

I looked at him with his chin resting in his hands and his head down, and I decided, with all the heartache Henry was going through because of Grandma's Bible, I should let him in on my little secret.

"Henry, what would ya say," I continued, "if I tol' ya that findin' those hog bandits is even more important than ya think?"

"Oh yeah," Henry said, not sounding at all excited. "Why's that?"

"Because, not only will we be savin' folks' hogs from those big, bad hog bandits," I explained, "but on top of that, findin' those hog bandits might lead us to savin' the entire Okefenokee Swamp!"

"What are ya talkin' 'bout, Elsie?" Henry asked, not sounding like he cared one tiny, little bit.

"Well, everyone's real worried on accounta that ship

canal somebody's wantin' to build through the Okefenokee,"
I explained. "And ya see, I wrote this letter to the president
'bout how he should stop the canal in order to save the swamp.
Well, my picture landing up in the newspaper fer capturin'
those hog bandits is gonna be jus' the thing to make the president pay attention to my letter. And when he does, he's gonna
save the whole swamp, and it'll all be cuz of me. Well, I mean
cuz of us."

Henry still didn't get excited. Maybe he didn't believe
me. But I didn't care either way. We were on our way to
Hollow Log Pond, and with each push of the boat pole, we
were getting closer to maybe finding those bandits.

The air around us got darker and cooler as we moved
deeper and deeper into the swamp. My heart pounded in my
chest. But unlike this morning when—at the thought of all those
hungry gators waiting in the water for Henry and me—my
blood had pumped fear into my veins, now it was different. Now it was pure excitement running through me at the
thought of where the danger in Hollow Log Pond might lead.

But as my heart raced with the anticipation of it all,
Henry's face told me his guilt over our disobedience was
sinking in the swamp and the fear he'd felt on our first visit to
Hollow Log Pond was filling its place.

Once we made it all the way into the pond, it felt even darker and colder than it had the last time we'd been there. Goose bumps covered my arms as Henry whispered his prayers. Even Huck wasn't in his usual dazed stupor. Instead he was sitting up, looking around, with his nose in the air.

Then, as if we were living the same moment all over again, a rustling in the bushes at the side of the pond broke the secluded silence.

Huck's ears perked up, and when I looked at Henry, he whispered, "Let's git outta here, Elsie Mae."

My heart banged inside me.

Hearing the sound again meant that most likely Grandpa had been wrong. The fellas who shot at us weren't just hunters lost in the woods. If they were, they wouldn't still be rustling around in here.

Could it be that this really was the hog bandits' hideout?

"We've got to figure out who's over there," I whispered back.

Henry realized that I had no intention of leaving without first trying to figure out a few things, so he went back to his rocking and praying. I guess he thought he had a better chance of God listening to him than of me listening to him.

We needed a plan, and we needed one quick before

anyone started shooting at us again. But I couldn't get my head around any good ideas.

Then the rustling sound came again, and this time it was followed by a muffled squeal.

Huck stood up and clawed at the boat underneath him.

I looked at Henry, and he opened his eyes.

I mouthed to him without making a sound, "That sounded like a hog."

Henry looked back at me with fear in his eyes. Probably because he was thinking what I was thinking. It was one thing to *think* the hog bandits *might* be hiding out here, but it was another to believe that they really *were* hiding out here. Both of us knew a couple low-downs stealing hogs wouldn't take too kindly to a couple kids stumbling upon their hiding place. It meant we could be in real danger. After all, last time they'd shot off a gun.

I squinted toward where the sound came from, trying to get a glimpse of the hog or the bandits, but it was too dark and the trees and bushes were just too thick. We hadn't heard any voices this time, so I wondered if maybe the bandits weren't back in the bushes. Maybe they had just hidden a hog there and were coming back later to get it.

By now, Henry was back to rocking and praying with

his eyes closed, so I knew he wouldn't be much help unless he really could get us some help from God. But since I didn't have nearly as much faith as Henry, even with my baptism just a few hours ago, I decided I'd better think of something on my own.

When one of Uncle Owen's hunting dogs got lost, he howled to call out to him, and last summer he had taught me how to howl. Maybe if I howled now, and the bandits heard me, they'd call out to see who was nearby. Henry and I wouldn't answer, but it would give us time to get out of there quick. If nobody called out after my howl, we'd know the bandits had left Hollow Log Pond.

"*Howwww! Howwwww!*" I howled.

Henry opened his eyes and shot daggers at me, obviously terrified that my howling would cause both of us to be caught just like all those missing hogs. But as my howl echoed off the water, a loud silence followed.

Huck climbed down off the front seat and stood in the bottom of the boat at my feet. I felt his anxiety through the thick folds of his skin as he brushed up against me.

"Henry," I whispered. "The bandits must be gone, but I bet they'll be back fer that hog sometime real soon. Let's rescue it and bring it home with us."

"Elsie Mae, we're playin' with danger here," Henry whispered back. "Let's jus' go back and tell Uncle Zeke. Then he can come over here with Uncle Owen and Uncle Lone, and the three of 'em can git that hog."

"It might be gone by then," I spat back. "We can't take that chance."

"*We* might be gone if we take that chance, Elsie Mae," Henry said. "We gotta jus' git outta here."

"I'm not leavin' without that hog," I said stubbornly. "Yer always sayin' the Lord protects the righteous. Well, rescuin' a hog and bringin' it home is 'bout the most righteous thing a person can do."

"Lord, have mercy on us," Henry wailed to himself.

I pushed on the pole, steering the boat over to the north side of the pond. As I squinted in the damp darkness, I sure hoped I wasn't wrong about those bandits being gone. Maybe they hadn't answered my howl because they were watching Henry and me, waiting for just the right time to add us to their hog bounty. The closer we got to the edge of the pond, the harder my heart pounded and the more earnestly Henry prayed. Just when my heartbeat felt louder than a drum, I saw movement in the thick shrubs just ahead of us. Then the rustling sounds came again, along with another squeal.

Henry shot me a terrified look.

I whispered, "We're both 'bout to become great big heroes."

I hoped my words, which I wasn't sure even *I* believed, would give us both some courage.

"More likely we're both 'bout to head home to gloryland," Henry whined in a worried voice.

And I don't know if it was my wishful thinking or Henry's mention of gloryland, but a sliver of sunshine somehow forced its way through the thick trees. That's when I finally saw it. It was an itty-bitty piglet. She was in the middle of a clump of tree branches that had been wedged around her to keep her captive, and a yellow handkerchief muzzled her tiny snout.

"It's a piglet, Henry!" I said in an excited whisper.

And Henry breathed a huge sigh of relief and whispered a heartfelt "Hallelujah!"

Now we had to figure out how to get her in the boat.

I knew the ground around Hollow Log Pond was soft and squishy. Uncle Owen had told me plenty of stories about people practically getting sucked to the center of the earth in places like this, so I was thankful Henry was back to rocking and praying. If I was going to rescue this piglet, the grace of God might be the only reason I didn't get swallowed alive.

I decided I'd do something I'd seen Uncle Owen do once when he had to rescue one of his hunting dogs that had gotten hurt and was stranded on the edge of Mirror Lake. I took the boat pole and laid it on the ground between the boat and the piglet. When Henry felt the boat tip to one side as I leaned over to lay down the pole, he opened his eyes. The look on his face made it clear that he trusted God a whole lot more than he trusted me.

Huck now stood on the middle seat of the boat right next to me, so I whispered, "Stay!"

And when Henry watched me carefully step out of the boat and onto the pole and reach for one of the branches of a nearby tree to steady myself, the look on his face told me, he not only didn't trust me, he actually thought I'd lost my mind.

"Oh, Lord we need ya now," Henry wailed as Huck's agitation caused the boat to sway side to side.

As I inched my way along the pole, it sank further and further into the squishy ground, but I made myself lighter by pulling hard on the branches around me as I steadied myself. Once, I finally reached the fence of tree branches that held the piglet captive, I scooted a little further along the pole so I could reach inside the clump of trees where the piglet stood.

The poor little thing must've been all worn out from fighting to get that muzzle off because when I reached out for her so I could untie the handkerchief, she didn't squeal or squirm or anything.

She couldn't walk on the pole to get back to the boat, so I had to carry her. I held her like I would've held Huck if he were a puppy. I walked backward on the pole. I carried her in one arm like a baby and used my other hand to steady myself with the nearby branches as I shuffled myself closer and closer to the boat. It was slow going, but I finally made it.

"*Hallelujah!*" Henry exclaimed as I stepped into the boat and handed the piglet to him while Huck sniffed and nudged at our new passenger.

I leaned over and pried the boat pole out of the muddy ground it was buried in.

"We gotta git out of here as fast as we can!" I said to Henry.

"Amen to that!" he agreed as he rubbed the piglet's head and rocked her like she was a newborn baby.

I pushed with all the strength I had left to head us out of the darkness of Hollow Log Pond, and as we made our way further and further into the bright sunshine, the realization of what we'd just done filled me with about as much pride as one person can hold. I was on my way to becoming the hero I had always wanted to be.

Chapter 20

Grandpa!" I yelled. "Grandpa!"

And even though I yelled at the top of my lungs, the piglet, which was now fast asleep in Henry's arms, slept so hard she didn't even stir.

As scared as Henry had been, and as much as he hadn't wanted to go back to Hollow Log Pond, I could tell as I looked at him sitting there in the boat, cradling that piglet, that he was feeling pretty, darn proud to be part of all this.

"Stay here, Henry," I said, jumping out of the boat and dragging it partway up the landing. "I'll run on up and git Grandpa."

Huck and I took off up the trail.

Before I even got to the front gate, I looked up and saw Grandpa hurrying down the trail.

"What's all the ruckus 'bout, Elsie?"

"We found a piglet, sir" I said excitedly. "In Hollow Log Pond, and it's gotta be those hog bandits that hid her there."

"Ya pullin' my leg, Elsie Mae?!" Grandpa exclaimed.

"No, sir! It's true!" I said. "C'mon!"

I turned back toward the landing, and Grandpa followed me.

When we got to the swamp's edge, Grandpa saw Henry holding the sleeping piglet.

"Well I'll be doggoned!" Grandpa exclaimed, laughing. "Or I guess I should say *hoggoned*!"

He walked into the shallow, muddy water and reached over and scooped up the sleeping piglet. She snuffled and stirred some, but then she settled right back down to sleep in the crook of Grandpa's arm.

"I think this might be Hamp's," Grandpa said, cradling the small animal in his big arms like it was a baby doll. "He jus' tol' me yesterday he was missin' one of his babies."

"Elsie and Henry," Grandpa said, sounding serious, "I'm gonna go on up and put her in the pen with our hogs till Owen or Lone and I can take her over to Hamp's, and then I want the two of ya to come on up to the porch and tell me everythin' that happened."

140

Grandpa walked away, and Henry and I looked at each other like we'd both just won a big old prize.

"I tol' ya all would be fergiven," I said.

"Well it worked out this time, Elsie Mae, but we can't go makin' a practice outta disobeyin' our elders," Henry said, standing up and leaping out of the boat onto the swamp's edge.

Even with his warning, I knew he was glad he'd let me lead him astray because I could tell he felt as good as I did that we were going to be getting a lot of attention for rescuing that hog.

"C'mon, Huck," I said as I slapped my leg, commanding Huck to follow me as I walked up the trail with Henry.

By the time we got up to the house, Grandpa was coming back around to the front of the house, so we all climbed the porch steps together, even Huck.

"Sarah," Grandpa called through the screen door. "Git on out here."

The screen door squeaked open and slapped shut behind Grandma as she came out of the door wiping her hands on her apron.

"What's goin' on, Zeke?" she asked.

"These young'uns got a story to tell," Grandpa said. "Take a seat."

Grandpa sat in one of the porch rocking chairs, and Grandma sat in the other. Henry and I stood in front of them, leaning back on the porch railing.

"So tell us what happened," Grandpa said.

"Well…" I started.

Now that we were here about to tell the story, I wasn't exactly sure where to begin. The very first thing Henry and I had done was disobey what Grandpa had said about not going back to Hollow Log Pond. I had told Henry all would be forgiven, but there was a little bit of doubt creeping into my mind.

"We were out in the boat," I said stalling. "And we were goin' 'long…"

"Uncle Zeke," Henry said. "First we have a confession to make."

What was Henry doing? This wasn't the way I wanted to start our hog rescue story.

"Ya see, sir," Henry continued. "We disobeyed ya and went back to Hollow Log Pond."

My insides groaned. I sure hoped Henry didn't mess this up for us.

Grandma looked confused, but Grandpa said, "Well, I kinda figured that, son."

Oh whew! Grandpa wasn't going to make a big deal

about us going back to the pond. He understood. Without us even telling our story, he had realized it was Hollow Log Pond that led us to finding that lost piglet.

"So, we went back there to look for clues that might lead us to the hog bandits," I jumped in, taking over the telling of the story. "Because I jus' had this feelin' in my gut that those fellas who shot at us the other day were the hog bandits."

"Shot at ya!" Grandma exclaimed. "Zeke, what is Elsie Mae talkin' 'bout? Have these young'uns been in harm's way?"

"Oh no, Grandma," I said. "We're fine. Henry's been prayin' the whole time."

"Yes, ma'am," Henry said. "The Lord protects those he loves."

"Sarah," Grandpa said, turning to Grandma, "Those men weren't shootin' at these two. They was probably jus' tryin' to scare 'em away. Now go on, Elsie."

"Well, so we went back to look fer clues," I continued, "And when we got there, we heard something rustlin' in the bushes. First, we thought it was those scoundrels again, but then we heard somethin' that sounded like squealin'. I had an inklin' it might be a hog, but I knew before we tried to do any rescuin', we needed to make sure the bandits weren't anywhere nearby."

"How'd ya do that?" Grandpa asked.

I looked over at Grandma before I answered and saw horror and shock all over her face. Even so, I continued with the story, hoping our happy ending would put her mind at ease. "I used the dog howl Uncle Owen taught me last summer. I figured if the bandits were nearby and heard the howl, they'd call out to see who was there."

"Elsie," Grandpa said, "that was a right smart thing ya did."

My heart filled with so much pride I thought it might explode like Henry had almost done the night he arrived in that too-small suit of his.

"Right smart thing!" Grandma gasped. "Are ya addled, Zeke?"

"Let's jus' let Elsie finish, Sarah," Grandpa said.

So I went on, "When no one answered the dog howl, we poled over to where the squeal was comin' from and saw the piglet, so we rescued her and brought her home."

I looked over at Henry. He still looked a little worried that we might get in trouble for the disobeying part, and it made me feel a tiny bit sorry for him. It must be hard to be so worried all the time about being good. I also felt a little guilty because the way I was tellin' the story, it seemed as if having

Henry there wasn't really all that important, but I knew in my heart of hearts that, even with my mind set on finding those bandits, if Henry hadn't been there, I likely wouldn't have had the courage to go back to Hollow Log Pond myself.

"Henry's prayers helped a lot, sir," I added.

"Well, the two of ya did a darn good thing bringin' that piglet home," Grandpa said. "And a mighty brave one too."

I looked at Henry, and I saw his guilt turn to relief that melted right into happiness.

"Ya *must* be addled in the brain, Zeke!" Grandma exclaimed. "These two could've gotten themselves kilt out there, and all under our care. And here ya go encouragin' 'em."

"They done a right good thing, Sarah," Grandpa said firmly.

"Right good thing," Grandma mumbled as she got up from the rocking chair and reached for the screen door. "Right good thing if ya want to end up gettin' shot at again."

Grandma went inside still muttering to herself.

"Don't ya pay her no mind," Grandpa said. "She'll git over it, and when she does, she'll realize she's as proud of ya as I am."

Chapter 21

Grandpa was wrong about Grandma realizing she was as proud of us as he was. By suppertime, Grandma had realized she was even *more* proud of us than Grandpa, and the meal she cooked proved it.

Usually supper was just leftovers from dinner, but tonight there were baked sweet potatoes, fried fish, Irish potato salad, snap beans from the garden, and there was more cornbread in the breadbasket than Grandma had made all summer. The only thing better than all that was the huckleberry pie sitting up next to the sink that I knew was our dessert.

"What's all this?" Uncle Lone asked as he sat down. "Looks like a feast."

"Jus' a meal fer our heroes," Grandma said, sitting down

and smoothing out her apron as she scooted herself closer to the table.

Uncle Owen winked at both Henry and me and said, "And I was happy to have the honor and pleasure of providin' the jackfish fer this here heroes' meal. They was jus' caught a coupla hours ago."

"Heroes, humph," Uncle Lone snorted, grabbing the square of cornbread that balanced at the top of the heap. "Jus' a stroke of luck these two found Hamp's piglet. Be the one to catch the bandits, like I aim t'do, and then y'all be *real* heroes."

"Oh, hush up, Lone!" Grandma scolded. "Or you'll be eatin' out on the porch. What these young'uns done t'day was noble and brave."

Both Henry and I sat up a little straighter and smiled at each other, and Uncle Lone took a bite out of his cornbread.

"Boy, spit that out right now!" Grandma scolded again. "We say grace 'round this house now, don't we, Henry? We need to thank the Lord fer all these blessin's," she said, nodding to the food on the table, "And even more fer keepin' these young'uns safe from harm's way t'day."

Henry, Uncle Owen, and I giggled while Uncle Lone spat his mouthful of cornbread onto his plate.

"Henry," Grandpa said. "Go on."

"Yes, sir," Henry said.

We all bowed our heads and folded our hands.

"Our Lord in Heaven, we praise yer name and thank ya fer yer bountiful blessings."

The smell of those bountiful blessings on the table was making me just about drool, so I prayed silently for Henry to hurry up.

"We're ever grateful fer yer constant protection on us. 'Specially on Elsie Mae and me as we stared into the face of danger t'day."

Amen to that, I thought.

"Help us not to become prideful of our accomplishments and good deeds."

Not become prideful? What was Henry talking about? What good was being a hero if you couldn't be prideful?

"Watch over our loved ones, Lord, wherever they might be."

Henry's voice wavered and cracked a little. He was still missing his mama and daddy.

Henry's prayer about not being prideful and the sad, lonely sound in his voice when he mentioned "loved ones" made me think if he didn't hurry up and finish praying, our moment of glory would sink to the bottom of the swamp the same way Grandma's Bible would have if I hadn't caught it in the nick of time.

So I counted my blessings when Henry finally said, "And keep us ever near to ya. Amen."

As soon as I opened my eyes, I saw Uncle Lone stuff the rest of the cornbread he had tried to eat a few minutes earlier into his mouth. He smiled at all of us as he chewed.

"Lone Marshall," Grandma said, "yer as impossible as keepin' a fly from a fresh jar of honey."

"It's jus' cuz I'm so sweet, Mama," Uncle Lone said grinning even wider.

"She's sayin' yer the pesky fly," Uncle Owen said, "not the sweet honey."

Uncle Lone stopped smiling, and we all laughed.

"Oh, don't start yer poutin'," Grandma said. "We all love ya even though ya's pesky. We wouldn't want ya any other way."

And as we all began to pass food around, Uncle Lone's smile came back. As I looked across the table at Henry, I was glad for all the laughter and good-natured teasing because it seemed to me that anything sorrowful Henry had thought about while he was praying had floated off to heaven with his prayers.

While we all piled our plates full, Uncle Owen said,

"So we went back to Hollow Log Pond and waited fer those low-down, no-good fellers fer a good while, but they never come back."

"I'm figurin' the scoundrels come back and saw us and took off again," Grandpa said. "Pretty sure they won't be comin' back to that pond no more. They's smarter than that. Look at how many hogs they stole and ain't been caught."

"I jus' wanted more 'n anythin' to find 'em there t'day and drag 'em into the sheriff," Uncle Owen said.

I had wanted more than anything to go back to Hollow Log Pond with Grandpa and Uncle Owen when they had gone looking for those bandits. But Grandma said she was plenty proud, but not at all addled. So, Henry, Huck, and I had to stay home.

But the bandits hadn't been at the pond, which meant they were still out in the swamp somewhere just waiting to be found, and I had my heart set on being the one to find them. And when I did, no matter what Henry James said, I planned on being plenty prideful about it.

I took a huge bite of warm cornbread and followed it with a spoonful of Irish potato salad, and the taste was just about as satisfying as knowing that Grandma had fixed all this special food on accounta us rescuing that piglet.

"You ain't gonna find those bandits by sittin' 'round waitin' fer 'em," Uncle Lone said. "Yer gonna have to catch 'em in the act."

"Yeah, and how ya aimin' t'do that?" Uncle Owen asked. "Havin' everyone sit up all night long watchin' their hog pens waitin' fer 'em to strike? Folks've been doin' that, and still there's missin' hogs."

"All right, y'all," Grandma said. "Can't we jus' take a rest from all this hog bandit jibber-jabber and enjoy the fact that we got two heroes livin' right here with us?"

"Yer mama's right, boys," Grandpa said. "In fact, why don't we have Elsie Mae and Henry James tell us again 'bout how they rescued that piglet. Lone hasn't heard the whole story yet, so, Elsie, why don't ya tell it from the beginning."

Uncle Lone grunted as he chewed.

I knew listening to our story was the last thing Uncle Lone wanted to do, but I swallowed the big bite of fried fish I had in my mouth and started the story that I couldn't wait to tell again. And as I did, everyone around the table continued to devour the feast Grandma had made in our honor until the serving platters were almost empty and our stomachs were so full they couldn't hold even one more bite.

Chapter 22

The next morning, Grandpa and Uncle Owen were headed over to Hamp's to bring back his piglet and to organize a couple search parties. Uncle Lone was supposed to go with them, but they didn't know where he was, and they couldn't wait anymore, so they were getting ready to leave without him.

As they got into Grandpa's boat, I asked one more time, "Why can't I go with ya? I'll be good, I promise."

"Elsie, yer grandma's right," Grandpa said. "It's too dangerous. We don't know what these bandits might do."

Uncle Owen sat in the middle seat holding Hamp's piglet. He gave me a sympathetic look, but I knew he couldn't give me permission if Grandma and Grandpa didn't want me to go.

I knew Henry didn't care about going along, but I wanted to go more than anything. The thing was, I didn't just *want* to go, I *needed* to go. Staying back on Honey Island while they went and captured those hog bandits was never going to make me the kind of hero I really wanted to be *or* get my picture in the newspaper.

Grandpa headed the boat up the waterway toward Minnies Island where Hamp lived. And as I watched the boat move away from the shore, Grandpa turned back toward me.

I hoped maybe he was going to change his mind, but instead he said, "And you and Henry don't go any farther than Billys Lake t'day. And stay away from Hollow Log Pond!"

I sighed. How would I have any chance of finding the bandits if I couldn't go out searching for them?

I headed up the trail to see where Henry and Huck were. As I got closer to the house, I could hear Henry practicing his preaching.

"And by his faith he was healed!" Henry exclaimed.

Once I made my way to the front gate, I saw Henry on the porch standing at the railing. Because of us ripping that page out of Grandma's Bible, Henry hadn't had the courage to borrow it again. But not being able to use the Bible hadn't stopped Henry from continuing to preach. He already knew a lot of scripture by heart, so he just practiced the same passages over and over.

Thankfully, Grandma hadn't noticed the torn page yet. With Henry quoting scripture and preaching and praying all the time, she didn't really need to read her Bible, so it would likely be a long time before she discovered the damage we'd done.

Before I got all the way up to the porch, I saw Uncle Lone coming around from the back of the house.

"What's with 'im?" Uncle Lone asked, nodding toward Henry standing at the porch railing.

"The Lord bless you and keep you…"

"He's jus' practicing, ya know, to be a preacher like his daddy."

"Yeah, his daddy's a real preacher all right," Uncle Lone said sarcastically. "And I'm a Sunday school teacher."

How did Uncle Lone stay so ornery all the time? Grandpa and Uncle Owen were probably glad he'd been late this morning, so they could leave without him.

"Grandpa and Uncle Owen jus' left fer Hamp's," I said. "They waited on ya as long as they could, but finally said they had to jus' go without ya."

"I ain't goin' over to Hamp's," Uncle Lone said, sounding annoyed. "All's I need is a search party of one."

I didn't know how Uncle Lone was so sure he would be the one to find the hog bandits, but I guess it was the same as me thinking maybe I could be the one to find them.

"I wanted to go with 'em," I said. "But they wouldn't let me."

"Ya got more trouble than hog bandits," Uncle Lone said.

"What do ya mean?" I asked.

"That dog of yers is out back pullin' laundry off the line," Uncle Lone said.

"Again?" I said, heading around the side of the house.

"Tol' ya that dog would be nothin' but trouble," Uncle Lone called after me, laughing.

When I got to the back of the house there were clothes scattered everywhere—two of Grandma's dresses covered the row of watermelons in the garden, one of Grandpa's shirts hung from the chicken yard fence, and another one lay draped over the hog pen gate. Huck lay in the shade with a pair of Grandpa's overalls in his mouth.

"What are ya tryin' t'do, Huck?" I hissed as I walked over and pried the overalls out of his mouth, hoping for two things—that there weren't any teeth marks on them and that Huck's slobbery drool wouldn't leave a stain.

I looked around the yard and wondered how Grandma hadn't seen this yet. Yesterday I'd been a hero, and today I'd be getting scolded worse than Uncle Lone. I hurried to collect the clothes and get them back up on the clothesline, hoping that by some miracle I'd be able to finish before Grandma saw the mess.

When I looked at the clothesline after I was finished, I thought about asking Henry to say a little prayer that Grandma wouldn't notice how crooked the clothes were. It was easy to see by looking at them that Grandma hadn't hung them. She was sure to figure out what had happened.

"C'mon, Huck," I said, calling him to follow me. "Let's git outta here while we can. Maybe if we're not 'round when Grandma comes outside to take in the laundry, we won't catch it fer messin' with her clean clothes."

Huck and I headed past Grandma's garden toward the side of the house, and that's when I saw one more thing lying on the ground, a rag. I must've missed something. But when I got closer, I realized it couldn't have been part of Grandma's laundry because it was still dirty. It was the kind of rag Grandpa, Uncle Lone, and Uncle Owen kept in their pockets every day to wipe off their hands after washing them or to dab the sweat off their forehead while they worked.

Huck sniffed at the rag, and then he started doing his crazy dance, sniffing the ground like he was following an invisible line. He sniffed and walked, sniffed and walked, sniffed and walked. I picked up the dirty rag and followed him. He meandered around the side of the house and out to the front where Henry was still practicing.

"And the Lord's mercy will be our constant hope!"

Uncle Lone sat in the rocking chair on the porch right behind Henry.

"And yer preachin' will be our constant annoyance," Uncle Lone mumbled.

"Lone Marshall! If ya don't stop that teasin' talk, and I have to come out there," Grandma's voice yelled from the kitchen, "yer gonna be sorry!"

Henry ignored Uncle Lone's teasing and Grandma's scolding and began to sing, "'Bind us together, Lord, bind us together with cords that cannot be broken...'"

As Henry sang, I kept watching Huck wind his way around the yard in front of the house, and I had a feeling I knew where he'd end up. I had a feeling that any minute, Huck and Uncle Lone would be bound together in a way that would mean something altogether different than the song.

Huck sniffed harder. Huck walked faster. He headed for the porch steps. Then he barreled up both steps. He leaped up onto Uncle Lone. The rocking chair tipped sideways. It landed on the porch with a crash. Uncle Lone went with it.

"*What in tarnation is this dog doin'!*" Uncle Lone yelled as he tried to push Huck and his slobbery tongue away from his face.

"What in heaven's name is goin' on out there!" Grandma yelled from inside.

"Lord, have mercy!" Henry exclaimed, turning around.

I ran up the porch steps and grabbed Huck around the neck, pulling him off Uncle Lone.

Uncle Lone wiped some of Huck's drool off his chin.

"Elsie Mae!" he said, sitting up and putting the rocking chair right ways up again. "I intend to put that dog where he shoulda been put when we found 'im."

"He was jus' tryin' to give ya the rag that dropped outta yer pocket," I said, holding out the dirty rag we'd found on the ground in the back of the house.

Grandma pushed the screen door open.

Huck still danced around, trying to get closer to Uncle Lone. I kept one arm around him, protecting him from Uncle Lone's wrath.

"Jus' like he was tryin' to bring in the laundry?" Uncle Lone asked, hoping to get Huck and me into more trouble.

"There ain't nothin' wrong with the laundry," I said, praying Grandma wouldn't look around the house and see how crooked the clothes were.

"Lone Marshall!" Grandma said, putting her hands on her hips. "Why don't ya go on back up to yer place and leave these young'uns alone? Ya shouldn't be shim-shackin' on the porch in the middle of the day anyway. 'Specially when yer brother and pa 'r' out there tryin' to track down those hog bandits."

"Loafin' 'round!" Uncle Lone exclaimed, standing up. "I've been doin' more'n anyone tryin' to find those scrapers."

I did kind of wonder why, if Uncle Lone had his heart so set on finding those hog bandits, he was wasting away his time in Grandpa's rocking chair.

"Well then, I think all this is addlin' yer brain," Grandma said. "Go on home and git some rest."

Uncle Lone glared at me. He grabbed his rag and stomped down the porch steps and headed toward the trail in the back of the house that led to the cabin where he and Uncle Owen lived.

"That boy, sometimes," Grandma said as she pulled the screen door open to let herself back inside. "Why don't y'all go on and find somethin' t'do too," she said to Henry and me. "I'll likely have to hold dinner till later this afternoon with Grandpa and Uncle Owen out there searchin' fer those hog bandits."

As she went back inside, I heard Grandma mumble to herself, "Be glad when this whole hog bandit thing is over. Ya ask me, it's got everyone's brain addled."

"Henry, c'mon," I said, jumping down from the porch without even using the steps. "We jus' got an answer to our prayers."

Henry and Huck both followed me as I headed for the trail toward the swamp's edge.

"Elsie Mae," Henry called. "Wait up!"

By the time he and Huck got down to the landing, I was already in the boat.

"Git in and let's go," I said. "I know how we're goin' to find those hog bandits."

Huck climbed in as soon as he saw me with the pole in my hand. He had grown to love riding in Uncle Owen's boat as much as I did. Henry was a different story.

"What do ya mean?" Henry asked. "Where we goin'?"

"Back to Hollow Log Pond," I said. "But we gotta hurry."

"Oh no!" Henry wailed. "I'm *definitely* not going back

to Hollow Log Pond. First, because I already kept up my end of the bargain and went back there again with ya once. Second, because Uncle Zeke told us not to. And third, because it's a sin to disobey yer elders."

Why did everything with Henry have to be so complicated?

"Henry, we *have* to go," I said. "We've been given a sign."

"What sign?" Henry asked.

"Well, actually not one sign, but three," I said. "I think Huck's special, and his nose fer findin' things is a gift from God."

I wasn't sure how far I should push this, but I really needed to convince Henry as quickly as I could to come with me.

"God's tryin' to tell us we need to use Huck to find the bandits," I said, hoping that squeezing the shape of the truth wasn't exactly the same as lying.

"Elsie…" Henry said.

"No, really, Henry," I said. "He's not jus' an ordinary dog. Ya know how Huck jus' jumped up on Uncle Lone the way he jumped up on Aunt Minnie and the way he jumped up on you that day in the garden when you was holdin' Grandma's Bible?"

"Yeah?"

"Well, that's his gift," I said.

"Jumpin' on people and lickin' 'em half to death is a gift from God?" Henry asked.

"No, not that," I said. "How he finds the people is his gift."

"What do ya mean?"

"Well, when Huck finds somethin' that belongs to someone, that somethin' smells like the person who lost it. Huck uses that smell to find those people. Then, when he finds 'em, he jumps on 'em, licks 'em, and slobbers 'em half to death."

"Ya mean jus' like when Uncle Owen's huntin' dogs find coons and possums, only Huck's nose helps 'im find people?"

"Yes!" I exclaimed, getting excited that I was finally getting through to Henry.

"I've heard 'bout dogs that can do that," Henry said. "But what 'bout the laundry?" he asked, still sounding skeptical. "If he's so special, why's he pullin' all the laundry off the line?"

I didn't have an answer to that. That was just Huck being Huck.

"I said he was special. I never said he was perfect."

Henry was silent for several seconds.

"Well, even if all that's true, what does that have t'do with us findin' the hog bandits? We don't have anythin' that smells like 'em."

"But if we go back to Hollow Log Pond, we might," I said, getting even more excited. "R'member how that piglet's snout was muzzled?"

"Yeah."

"Well, I took that handkerchief off her snout 'fore I brought her in the boat with us, and I bet it's still back there in Hollow Log Pond. All *we* have t'do is go back and git it. Then Huck can smell it and lead us right to the hog bandits."

I knew that handkerchief would also have a lot of piglet smell on it and probably a lot of other smells too, but I hoped that somehow enough of the low-down hog bandits' scoundrelly smell would still be on it—at least enough so that Huck could pick up their scent.

"And ya know what the best part is?" I asked, getting even more excited.

"What?" Henry said, sounding as if he was getting less excited with every word I said.

"Huck never yips or barks or growls, so when we do git him sniffin' the trail to those bandits, we'll be able to sneak up on 'em without makin' a sound."

"Elsie Mae," Henry said, making his voice sound as if he were preaching at a funeral, "that sounds as dangerous as playin' with dynamite."

"Yeah, but if we find those hog bandits, we'll be even bigger heroes than we were when we rescued that piglet," I said. "And that sounds 'bout as excitin' as watchin' fireworks."

"But, Elsie, 'the ways of the wicked lead to destruction,'" Henry said, sounding as somber as he could possibly be. "And this all sounds 'bout as wicked as can be."

"But, Henry, 'when ya help the least of these, ya help me,'" I said, hoping that of all those verses I'd learned in Sunday school, I would know the right ones to persuade Henry James that finding those hog bandits was part of God's plan for both of us.

Chapter 23

All the way up the waterway to Billys Lake and then through the narrow channel that led toward Hollow Log Pond, Huck slept, I poled, and Henry recited Psalm 23 in hushed whispers. The dark coolness of the deep swamp felt dangerous but welcoming as I thought about how close we might be to catching those hog bandits.

"Henry," I whispered. "Open yer eyes. We're here."

He sighed, opened his eyes, and then squinted in the darkness, looking for what might be lurking in between the trees. The damp and still, silent air pressed against my sweaty skin, making me feel clammy. Even though no one seemed to be around and the hog bandits were unlikely to come back here, I wanted to stay quiet just in case.

"I'll do the dog howl again," I whispered. "Jus' to be sure nobody's here."

My howl caused Huck to lift his head as my voice echoed over the water. We waited in the quiet that followed to see if anyone would answer, but no one called back to us.

"Looks like they're not here," I said. "Let's go look fer that handkerchief."

I pushed on the pole to guide us to the edge of the pond and the spot where I'd gotten out of the boat.

"I'm gonna have to git out and walk on my pole again to git a closer look back there," I said to Henry.

"Oh, Lord, have mercy on us," he whispered as he rocked back and forth.

Henry was his usual anxious self, but Huck had already put his head back down to rest again, so I wasn't too worried those hog bandits were anywhere nearby.

I pushed the boat up against the trees as far as I could. Then I laid the pole down on the ground, grabbed a couple branches to steady myself, and stepped out of the boat. I felt myself sink in the swampy muck.

"Lord, be near us now," Henry wailed.

I inched my way along, closer and closer to where we'd found the piglet. I scanned the mucky ground for something yellow, but I didn't see anything but sticks and vines and swampy mud.

"It's gotta be here somewhere," I said.

"Oh, Elsie," Henry said, looking around. "Let's jus' leave the search parties to find those ol' bandits. This is dangerous out here. 'Specially when we're not even supposed to be here."

I ignored Henry and kept inching along and looking around. I didn't see how that handkerchief could've disappeared, but after a few more minutes of walking on that skinny pole and holding myself up with nearby branches, I was getting tired. Maybe we wouldn't be able to find the handkerchief after all, which probably meant we wouldn't get to be the ones to find those hog bandits.

"Oh, all right," I finally said. "I guess it's not here."

I scooted myself back along the pole toward the boat.

"Don't worry, Elsie Mae. The Lord rewards the footsteps of the righteous," Henry said.

"I don't want a reward from the Lord, Henry," I said, getting back into the boat. "I want to be the one to find those hog bandits, and without that handkerchief, I don't have the clue I need."

Henry could tell I was mad, so he gave it a rest with all his wisdom from above.

I reached over to lift the boat pole out of the mud. It was really stuck this time, so I had to use a nearby stick to dig underneath it to pry it free. When I finally got it loose, I saw something sticking out of the muck underneath the stick.

It was yellow.

It was the corner of the handkerchief!

"Henry!" I yelled. "I found it! I found the handkerchief!"

He leaned over the side of the boat to see for himself.

"*Hallelujah!*" he yelled.

And Huck, who had already drifted off to sleep again, lifted his head to see what all the fuss was about.

I dug my fingernails into the mud to uncover the rest of the handkerchief.

"It must've fallen to the ground the other day and gotten buried when we rescued Hamp's piglet," I said, pulling the muddy handkerchief free from the swampy ground. "I sure hope it's still got 'nough of the hog bandits' smell on it."

"I'll start prayin' that it does, Elsie Mae," Henry said with a huge smile on his face. "Because with the Lord on our side and Huck's nose on the ground, I have faith that a miracle jus' might happen."

There was a piece of an old *Charlton County Caller* lying in the bottom of the boat. It was kind of soggy, but even so,

I used it to wrap up the handkerchief. I knew it had to have other smells on it by now, but maybe the newspaper would protect it from getting even more.

"We better git outta here, in case those low-downs come back," I said.

Using the muddy pole, I pushed us toward the water-way leading out of Hollow Log Pond.

"We'll need to make a plan for usin' that handkerchief to find those hog bandits," Henry said.

He was finally talking and thinking like I was. This was working out just fine. We had a real good chance of being the ones to find those hog bandits, which meant *I'd* have a real good chance of having my picture in the *Charlton County Caller*. And just like Henry James said, there might just be a miracle. President Roosevelt might save the Okefenokee Swamp after all. And it might just end up being all because of me.

As we made our way through the narrow channel toward Billys Lake, I said, "Now Henry, I don't think we should tell anyone else 'bout any of this jus' yet."

"Me either," Henry agreed. "Well, I'll be talkin' to the Lord 'bout it, of course, but that's it."

I smiled. Henry really was turning out all right.

Then just as we were almost out into the open water, I heard, "*Yeeeeowwwweeee! Yeeeowwwweee!*"

Henry looked at me with fear in his eyes. It was Uncle Owen's swamp call, and it sounded like he was coming from Billys Lake. I knew Henry had to be worried that Grandpa was going to be able to tell where we had just come from because I was a little worried about the same thing, especially since I didn't want to tell Grandpa about the handkerchief *or* our plan to use Huck to find those hog bandits.

As soon as our boat made it all the way out into the open, we could see Uncle Owen and Grandpa way at the far end of Billys Lake. Before they got close enough, I tried to position the boat so that it looked like we had just come from Honey Island, instead of Hollow Log Pond.

Once they got close enough, they waved, so I put down the forked stick, picked up the paddle, and headed toward them.

When we got a little closer, Uncle Owen yelled, "We got 'em! We caught the hog bandits!"

What?

After all that, Henry and I were too late?

"The Lord does *not* reward the disobedient," Henry said.

"Oh, hush up, Henry!"

As we paddled toward them, I could tell that there wasn't anyone else in Grandpa's boat with them.

"Where are they?" I yelled.

"Hamp and his son Farley's bringin' 'em in his boat," Grandpa called. "They're not far behind us."

"We're all meetin' up at our place and holdin' 'em there till we can git the sheriff to come out. We sent Hamp's oldest boy, Charlie, over to Traders Hill to fetch Sheriff Jones," Uncle Owen explained once they got close enough.

"Where'd ya find 'em?" I asked.

"In an old shack over on Pine Island," Uncle Owen said. "They was right out in the open, the darned fools."

"How'd ya know it was them?" Henry asked. "Did they confess?"

Of course Henry was concerned about their souls.

"They didn't have to," Grandpa said. "They was up there countin' their money."

"Money they made from sellin' swamp folks' hogs," Uncle Owen said.

"I've never *seen* so much money," Grandpa added.

"It's the root of all evil," Henry said sadly, but I could tell his sadness wasn't about the hog bandits' sinfulness.

I didn't care what verses Henry spewed out about

disobedience not being rewarded or pride going before the fall, he was just as disappointed as I was about us missing our chance to be the big heroes.

"Where've the two of you been?" Grandpa asked, suddenly sounding a little suspicious.

"Oh, jus'… ya know," I said. "Here and there."

I hoped I'd chosen words that wouldn't cause Henry to feel like he had to confess the *real* truth. If I kept my answer vague, maybe Henry would be able to just let it go, and luckily, I was right.

"Well, let's hurry and git on up to the house," Uncle Owen said. "I can't wait till Sheriff Jones gits there and arrests those scoundrels."

Chapter 24

Grandpa, Uncle Owen, Henry, and I all stood at the swamp's edge waiting for Hamp and Farley to show up with the hog bandits and for Charlie to show up with Sheriff Jones. Grandma was even there at the landing as we all anxiously watched the waterway that led to Honey Island. Oblivious to all the excitement, Huck still lay in the boat sleeping.

Before we saw anyone coming, we heard, "*Yowwweeeee! Yowwweeeee!*"

Hamp's swamp call.

A few minutes later, we saw his boat cutting through the smooth surface of the cypress-colored water. Hamp stood in the back of the boat paddling, and Farley sat in the middle seat with his shotgun, while two strangers sat next to each other in the front of the boat. Even from far away, I could tell their hands were tied behind their backs, and as soon as the boat got closer, I could tell they looked just exactly like what you'd think hog bandits would look like. They were dirty, their hair was long and snarly, and their clothes were ripped and torn.

I still couldn't believe Henry and I weren't the ones to find them.

"The sheriff here yet?" Hamp called.

"Not yet," Grandpa answered.

"Likely gonna take Charlie a bit to track down the sheriff and git 'im here," Uncle Owen said.

"Owen's right," Grandpa said as Hamp's boat slid up onto the landing.

All the while, those hog bandits were cussing like crazy, saying words I had never even heard before.

I felt my stomach quiver a little at the thought of how close Henry and I had been to catching these low-downs ourselves. One sideways look at Henry told me he was thinking the exact same thing.

"Don't even think 'bout tryin' any funny business," Farley said as he stood up in the boat so he could get out.

"You swamp folks don't scare us," one of the hog bandits grumbled in a nasty voice.

Now my stomach didn't just quiver; it trembled.

"I still got my shotgun," Farley said, stepping out of the boat, "and I ain't 'fraid to use it."

Hamp grabbed one of the hog bandits by the arm, and Farley grabbed the other. They stood them up and pulled them out of the boat.

"Let's git these two on up to the yard," Grandpa said. "We'll keep 'im tied up till Sheriff Jones gits here. Sarah can bring us some tea so's we can relax on the porch while we wait."

"I'd love to," Grandma said. "Elsie and Henry, why don't y'all c'mon up and help me?"

"C'mon, Huck," I said, slapping my leg.

Huck had woken up when Hamp's boat arrived, so when I called him, he shook himself and then loped over to follow Grandma, Henry, and me up the trail toward the house.

A few minutes later, Henry and I came out on the porch with the jars.

The two hog bandits already sat on a stump in the far corner of the yard with their hands still tied behind their backs. Farley stood next to them in the shade of one of the chinaberry trees with his shotgun at the ready. And as Grandpa, Uncle Owen, and Hamp made their way across the yard toward the porch, Grandma came through the screen door behind me with the tea.

"They still act like they don't know what they done," Hamp said as he sat down on the porch swing, taking the tea Grandma handed him. "All the way here they kept sayin', 'We don't know nothin' 'bout no hogs.' But I don't believe 'em. Look at 'em. They look jus' like criminals, don't they?"

Henry was standing next to me on the porch, and I imagine he wanted to say something about how God doesn't look at a man's outward appearance, only at his heart, but I knew he wouldn't say anything on accounta Hamp being his elder. It would've seemed disrespectful, and then Henry would just have one more sin to confess along with all the other ones I'd talked him into.

But I agreed with Hamp. They *did* look like criminals, and once they had gotten close enough to us down on the landing, they even *smelled* like criminals—like moonshine and sweat, just the way I thought a hog bandit would smell. And I would've bet my life that their insides didn't look *or* smell any better than their outsides.

"Don't matter," Uncle Owen said. "They ain't gotta admit to nothin' cuz the proof is right here."

He held up the cloth sack full of money Grandpa had taken from them.

Next thing we knew, Sheriff Jones came walking up the trail with Charlie.

"Here they come," Uncle Owen said.

And as Charlie opened the gate, all of us up on the porch went out into the yard to meet them.

Sheriff Jones was short and round and waddled as he walked toward us.

"Hi, y'all," he said, shaking hands with Grandpa, Hamp, Uncle Owen, and Farley.

Seeing Sheriff Jones reminded me of Uncle Lone and his sorted past, and I wondered for the first time where he was. I'd forgotten all about him until now. Maybe he'd heard that the bandits had been captured, and he was so disappointed that he hadn't been the one to catch them that he was off pouting somewhere. It was the first time I ever felt kind of sorry for Uncle Lone because I sort of felt like pouting too.

"We appreciate ya comin' out," Grandpa said.

"No problem," Sheriff Jones said. "These the guys?" he asked, nodding toward the stump where the bandits sat tied up.

I thought to myself that he must not be a very good sheriff if he had to ask which ones the criminals were when they were tied up right in front of him.

"Yup, and here's the proof," Uncle Owen said, handing him the bag of money.

"The heart of the honest man will prosper," Henry said.

I wasn't about to spout off verses like Henry, but it did make me mighty proud to think that Grandpa and Uncle Owen were giving that money to the sheriff. Lots of folks probably would've thought it rightly belonged to them after all the trouble we'd been going through around here. I wondered what Uncle Lone would've done with the money if he'd been the one to find the bandits. And then I wondered what *I* would've done if Henry and I would've been the ones to find them. But I knew if Henry had been with me, I really didn't have to wonder about that.

The sheriff walked over to where the hog bandits sat.

"You low-downs probly never thought ya'd get caught, did ya?" he said in disgust. "Most men work hard all day, but y'all go 'round stealin' other folks' hogs in the night like a coupla animals yerselves."

"We ain't stole no hogs!" one of them yelled.

"We don't even eat bacon!" the other one added, and the two of them laughed at the joke until their fit of laughter turned into sputtering spasms of coughing.

"Oh, we got a coupla funny boys, here, do we?" Sheriff Jones said and then spit at their feet. "We'll see how many jokes yer makin' when yer locked up in a jail cell with nothin' to eat and drink but bread and water."

This sheriff was starting to impress me a little now.

"Well, I'd like to thank ya kind gentlemen of the swamp fer catchin' these scoundrels," the sheriff said, turning to Grandpa and the other men. "I'll be glad to take 'em off yer hands."

"We'd be much obliged," Hamp said.

"Now what 'bout that reward you was offerin'?" the sheriff asked. "Who's the lucky son of a gun who gits to claim that?"

Grandpa, Uncle Owen, Hamp, Farley, and Charlie all smiled at one another and then looked at the sheriff.

"That money'll be goin' back to the good folks of the swamp who offered it up," Grandpa said. "The four of us already decided we don't need no reward."

"Yeah," Hamp added. "Knowin' our hogs is safe is reward 'nough. Charlie here'll go back to Traders Hill with ya to pick up that money, so we can return it to folks. Fact, Farley'll go 'long too so's ya got 'nough help keepin' an eye on those two scrapers."

"Y'all swamp folks are mighty kind, aren't ya?" Sheriff Jones said, smiling.

He turned and reached down to grab one of the hog bandits by the arm.

"How 'bout a little tea 'fore ya head back?" Grandma called from the porch, holding up the pitcher.

"That's mighty kind of ya, ma'am," Sheriff Jones said, letting go of the bandit's arm he held. "I think I'll take ya up on that."

"Farley, you stay here with yer shotgun," Hamp said as we all walked back up toward the porch where Grandma still stood with the tea.

"Yes, sir," Farley said.

The sheriff took the jar full of tea Grandma held out, and then sat in the rocking chair that Grandpa offered him.

"That's a mighty fine dog y'all got there," Sheriff Jones said, looking down at Huck who lay sleeping on the porch.

"He's mine," I said, climbing the porch steps and sitting down next to Huck so I could scratch his head while he slept. "His name's Huck."

"It looks to me like he's got some bloodhound in 'im," the sheriff said, and then he took a long drink of tea.

"I think that dog's got a li'l more than bloodhound in 'im," Grandma said, laughing. "He darn near gits into everythin' 'round here."

"Is that so?" Sheriff Jones asked and then took another long drink of tea, "*Aaahhhh!* Ain't nothin' like tea made from Okefenokee Swamp water, is there?"

"No, sir," Grandma said, smiling as if she herself had something to do with how good the water tasted.

I sure hoped Grandma would get to keep being proud of that water for a long time, but now that I hadn't been the one to catch the bandits, how would I ever make sure the president paid attention to my letter?

"By the way," Sheriff Jones said, getting up and handing his jar back to Grandma, "where'd ya git that dog anyways?"

"My uncle Lone found 'im," I answered, "and he gave 'im to me."

"Hmm," the sheriff said.

"Ya know, Sheriff, ya may have some competition fer yer job someday," Grandpa bragged. "It was Elsie Mae here and her cousin Henry who found one of our missin' hogs the other day."

"Is that right?" Sheriff Jones said, smiling at Henry and me. "Maybe the two of you 'ill be the next sheriffs in these parts."

He headed down the porch steps and back out to the yard. He reached down and grabbed the two hog bandits by their arms and led them toward the trail. Farley and Charlie followed them.

"I'm tellin' ya!" one of the bandits yelled. "We ain't stole no hogs!"

I watched the sheriff, the hog bandits, Farley, and Charlie as they disappeared down the trail.

And even though the hog bandit mystery that had loomed over the swamp all summer was finally over, I felt a bothersome little nagging in the middle of my stomach. But I sure couldn't put my finger on why.

Chapter 25

In the next few days, Henry and I had more fun together than we'd had all summer long. We built a lean-to in the woods behind Grandma and Grandpa's house. Uncle Owen took us fishing for an entire afternoon. I taught Henry how to pole the boat, and he was already getting pretty darn good at it. And even though Grandma didn't want him to, Grandpa took us coon hunting in the middle of the night with all four of Uncle Owen's hunting dogs.

In all our busyness and fun, Henry forgot all about his preaching, which I hoped helped him miss his mama and daddy a little less. And since no one was talking much about that ship canal, I figured maybe I could take a break from worrying about it for a while.

Henry and I were enjoying ourselves way too much to

spend any time playing church or fretting about something that might not even happen—or that might not be as bad as everyone was making it out to be, even if it did happen. But that all changed one morning while we were eating breakfast.

Henry had just finished saying grace when we heard a swamp call coming up from the shore.

"That sounds like Hamp," Grandpa said. "I wasn't expectin' 'im this mornin'."

We all scooted away from the table and headed outside. We walked down the porch steps toward the trail to the landing, anxious to know what Hamp was doing here. Before we made it to the swamp's edge, we saw him heading up toward us.

"What 'r' ya doin' up here so early?" Grandpa asked.

"Come to tell ya that our hog problem ain't over," Hamp said. "Lost 'nother one last night."

"What?" Uncle Owen exclaimed.

"Yep," Hamp said. "Went out early this mornin' to gather some eggs for Eva, and when I walked past our hog pen, I noticed right away our biggest hog's missin'."

"How did that happen when those scoundrels are sittin' in a cell over at Traders Hill?" Grandpa asked.

"Maybe they weren't the real hog bandits," I said.

"They *did* keep insistin' they was innocent," Henry added.

"Well, doesn't that jus' beat all," Grandma said. "Jus' when we thought our troubles was over."

This was bad news news for swampers and their hogs, but it was a turn of good fortune for Henry and me. If the hog bandits hadn't been caught yet, maybe we could still use Huck to help us catch them. I wondered if that handkerchief was still lying wrapped up in that newspaper at the bottom of the boat.

"Looks like we'll need to be organizin' some new search parties," Uncle Owen said.

"Well, y'all won't be doin' it on an empty stomach," Grandma said. "Those hog bandits can wait. I've got breakfast on the table. C'mon up to the house with us, Hamp, and join us fer somethin' to eat."

"Won't pass up a chance fer yer cookin', Sarah," Hamp said, grinning.

I tried to get Henry's attention by giving him a look, hoping he'd realize, like I did, that we'd just been given another chance at being heroes, but he didn't pay me no mind as we all walked back up to the house.

I knew Henry being oblivious to our good fortune was the least of my worries. What I really needed to worry about was how I was going to get him to go back to Hollow Log Pond with me.

"Take Lone's spot, Hamp," Grandpa said as we all shuffled around the table again. "He's been harder to find these days than those hog bandits."

"Yeah," Henry said. "Where *has* Uncle Lone been these last few days?"

"Oh, he's jus' cross cuz he wasn't in on the capture of the bandits the other day," Uncle Owen said. "Maybe when he finds out the real bandits are still out there, he'll cheer up a li'l at the thought of havin' another chance to maybe be the one to track 'em down."

I gave Henry another look, but he was too busy stuffing a spoonful of corn grits in his mouth to notice I was trying to get him to realize that with Huck and that handkerchief, we had a better chance than anyone of finding the real hog bandits.

"Well, I heard some good news the other day that might cheer everyone up," Hamp said, piling a huge heap of eggs on his plate.

"Well, some good news would be a nice change," Grandma said.

"Rumor has it that the ship company that wanted

to build that canal ain't gonna be able to step foot in the Okefenokee," Hamp said, smiling.

"Really?" I said.

"Yep, heard it when I was up in Waycross a coupla days ago," Hamp said.

"What a blessing!" Grandma said.

"That it is, but you wanna hear the best part?" Hamp asked.

"What?" I said, praying harder than Henry that by some miracle the best part would be that it was all because of me.

"People are sayin' that President Roosevelt 'imself had somethin' to do with it," Hamp said.

"Hallelujah!" I yelled.

Everyone looked at me like I had just turned into Henry James. Henry looked at me probably wondering how my letter had gotten the president's attention when our picture hadn't even ended up in the newspaper. But everyone quickly turned back to Hamp to hear what else he had to say.

"Yep, president's supposed to be gittin' all kinda laws passed that're gonna protect this here swamp, not jus' from that ship company, but from anyone who wants t'do any harm to the Okefenokee," Hamp explained. "Folks is sayin' it's a real mystery how the president done even found out our swamp needed savin'."

"I imagine as soon as it's official, we'll be readin' somethin' 'bout it in the *Charlton County Caller*," Hamp said.

"*Hallelujah!*" I yelled again even louder, almost falling off the bench Henry and I were sitting on.

This time, everyone looked at me like I was crazier than a hound dog trapped in a barn with a bobcat.

Could it really be that *my* letter had made the president want to save the swamp?

"Elsie Mae," Grandma said, "what's gotten into ya?"

Henry looked at me with folded hands and a bowed head. I'm sure he thought the only way this could've happened was through all *his* prayers, but I didn't care what he thought. All that mattered was that the president was saving the Okefenokee, and there was a darn good chance it was because of me! Even so, I still wanted to keep it a secret. That way it could be a great, big surprise when the truth came out.

"Jus' happy to hear the swamp'll be safe now," I said, scooting the bench underneath the table again.

Everyone looked at me like I was more addled in the brain than Uncle Lone.

Hamp's news was even bigger than hearing that the

hog bandits were still on the loose, just waiting for Henry and me to find them.

"Well, Hamp, that's some mighty good news ya brought us this mornin'," Grandpa said.

"*Yeeooooow! Yeeoooooow!*" cut through the kitchen, interrupting our celebration.

"That's Farley," Hamp said. "What in tarnation's he doin' up here? He's supposed to be back at our place helpin' Eva make a batch of her brown sugar for the frolic that's comin' up."

We all looked at one another in confusion.

We scooted out from the table again and all headed outside. This time, when we got down the porch steps, we saw Sheriff Jones and Farley coming through the gate.

"Sheriff showed up jus' after ya left, Pa," Farley explained when he saw how confused we all looked.

"Soon as I talked to yer boy," Sheriff Jones said, "I knew what I come to tell ya wasn't gonna be no surprise."

"Lemme guess," Uncle Owen said. "Ya found out those two low-downs ya got locked up ain't the real hog bandits after all."

"Darn right 'bout that," Sheriff Jones said as he pulled up the waistband on his pants that were sliding down his round stomach. "Found out from a coupla other scoundrels we brought in that those boys y'all caught the other day didn't get all that money stealin' hogs. They was runnin' moonshine."

"That's why they kept sayin' they never stole no hogs," Henry said.

"Yep," Sheriff Jones said. "But they'll be stayin' locked up right where they are. Their moonshine-runnin' days're over."

"But that doesn't solve our hog bandit problem," Uncle Owen said. "Does it?"

"Nope," the sheriff said. "And 'sides that, I'm 'fraid we got ourselves 'nother problem."

The sheriff looked around, and his eyes landed on Huck, who was sleeping under the swing on the front porch. That bothersome feeling in my stomach that I'd had several days ago, when Sheriff Jones left with the supposed hog bandits, pounced on me like Huck on a huckleberry pie.

"Oh yeah," Grandpa said. "What's that?"

"Done some checkin' the other day after I was out here," Sheriff Jones said. "Seems that the Pierce County Sheriff's Department up north of Waycross is missing a dog from their K-9 unit."

"What 'r' ya talkin' 'bout?" Uncle Owen asked.

"I'm talkin' 'bout that dog right up there," Sheriff Jones said, pointing at Huck.

"My brother and I found that dog abandoned and 'bout half-starved in the swamp weeks ago," Uncle Owen said.

"That's because he was lost on a rescue mission," the sheriff said. "The K-9 unit looked fer him as long as they could, and then they had to give up and go on back home.

"That dog lost his voice box in a rescue-related injury several months 'fore that, so they figured without 'im being able to bark or growl to protect 'imself, he was most likely dead. Maybe kilt by a wild animal or somethin'."

"Yeah, so?" Uncle Owen said.

"So, that dog there is a bloodhound mix, 'specially trained, and one of the best trackin' dogs in Pierce County," Sheriff Jones said, getting more stern with each word he spoke.

My heart pounded in my ears, and I ran up the porch steps, kneeled next to Huck, put my arms around his neck, and rested my chin on his head. I rubbed my hand against that big, lumpy scar, and now that I knew how it had gotten there, it just made me love Huck even more, which I didn't think was even possible.

"What 'r' ya sayin', Sheriff?" Grandpa asked.

"I'm sayin' that dog doesn't belong to y'all," Sheriff Jones said in a real matter-a-fact way.

"Well, *we're* sayin' that he does," Grandpa said in a real I'm-about-to-get-mad way.

"The girl's gonna have to give back that dog," Sheriff Jones said sternly.

I couldn't believe my ears. There was no way I could give up Huck.

"Well, Sheriff," Grandpa said sternly, taking a step closer to the sheriff and looking him straight in the eye. "Thank ya fer informin' us of all this, but if the Pierce County Sheriff's Department wants their dog back, first off, they're gonna have to prove that it's theirs, and last off, they're gonna have to wrestle me to get it. That dog belongs to Elsie Mae!"

With that, Grandpa turned away from Sheriff Jones and walked around to the back of the house.

I stared out at the sheriff from the porch. I still held on to Huck with both arms. I watched the sheriff turn and walk back down the trail toward the landing, and when he disappeared in the trees, I buried my head in the loose skin around Huck's neck and cried and cried.

Chapter 26

After Grandpa, Uncle Owen, and Hamp had gone over to Hamp's place to organize a meeting about searching for the hog bandits again, Henry sat on the swing behind Huck and me with his hand on my shoulder. I sat on the porch floor next to Huck.

"Elsie Mae," Henry said. "It's gonna be OK. Uncle Zeke won't let 'em take Huck away.

"Lord, comfort Elsie with yer love." Henry prayed over me like I was kneeling at the church altar instead of crying about losing my dog.

I finally lifted my head and wiped my face with the back of my hand. I turned and looked at Henry.

"We've gotta go find those hog bandits," I said in a croaky voice.

"What?" Henry asked.

"It might be the only way fer me to save Huck," I said. "Let's go!"

Henry knew not to argue with me in the sorrowful state I was in, so he followed me.

"C'mon, Huck," I yelled behind me as I hurried down the porch steps and slapped my leg.

Oblivious to all the heartache that was going on around him, Huck lifted his sleepy head, stood up, and loped down the steps after us.

When we got down to the swamp's edge, I saw the newspaper still lying in the bottom of Uncle Owen's boat. I grabbed it and unwrapped it, and thankfully, the handkerchief was still tucked safely inside. The three of us stepped into the boat and settled into our usual spots.

"Listen," I said to Henry. "First, we're goin' to head back to Hollow Log Pond."

"Oh, Lord, have mercy," Henry groaned. "I was 'fraid ya was gonna say that."

"Once we git there," I said as I pushed us away from the landing, "we're goin' to let Huck smell that handkerchief that we found the other day to git the scent of those bandits, and then we'll let him lead us right to 'em."

"Elsie Mae?" Henry asked. "Do ya really think that's a good idea?"

Henry already knew me well enough to know the answer to his question, so I didn't bother answering. I just turned the boat toward the waterway leading to Hollow Log Pond.

As the boat cut through the narrow passage that was becoming so familiar to Henry and me, he asked another question. "How ya figurin' findin' those hog bandits is gonna help ya keep Huck?"

"Well," I said, "I'm hopin' if we find the hog bandits, ol' Sheriff Jones will be so grateful to us fer what we done that he'll let me keep Huck as a reward."

Even as I said those words out loud, I felt my stomach scrunch up in a big old knot because I really wasn't sure the sheriff would do something like that. But what else could I do? If I didn't do anything, it might only be a matter of time before Sheriff Jones showed up again, this time with the Pierce County Sheriff's Department and proof of everything Sheriff Jones said. Then there'd be no hope of me hanging on to Huck.

We finally got to the pond, and it was as dark and as damp as it always was, but for some reason, the place didn't seem all that scary any more. Even for Henry. He wasn't rocking or praying or anything. He actually had his eyes wide open.

The thing was that I was a lot more afraid of losing Huck than of the dangers that might be lurking in Hollow Log Pond.

"OK, boy," I said, taking the handkerchief all the way out of the folded-up newspaper. "It's yer turn to be a hero."

Huck opened his sleepy eyes, but he didn't even lift his head.

"Do ya really think this'll work?" Henry asked.

I wasn't sure. Would Huck *really* be able to find the bandits? And if he did, would it *really* mean that I'd get to keep him?

Instead of answering Henry's question, I just said, "Maybe ya should jus' start prayin', Henry. We could use all the help we can git with this."

"Dear Lord, we know yer power is great," Henry began.

"Huck," I said, turning to put the handkerchief in front of his nose, "c'mon and smell this."

Huck just lay there and didn't seem at all interested. I wondered what the officers who trained Huck said when they wanted him to find someone. There had to be some sort of official command, but I sure didn't know what it was.

I kept the handkerchief under his nose and tried something else: "Go git 'im!"

And this time, Huck lifted his head and sniffed at the handkerchief, and I felt a flutter of excitement in my scrunched-up, worried stomach. After he sniffed, he stood up on the seat, lifted his head in the air, and sniffed.

"Henry!" I said, interrupting his prayers. "It's workin'. Huck smells somethin'."

We both looked at Huck and then at each other.

"Hallelujah!" Henry yelled. "My prayers've been answered!"

"OK, Henry," I said. "Yer gonna have to sit up front with Huck and somehow figure out which way he wants us to go, and I'll keep directin' the boat that way."

With his sniffing, Huck led us around the edge of Hollow Log Pond, but then he just kept leading us in the same direction, and we circled the pond again. Henry and I looked at each other and sighed. Maybe this wasn't going to work after all.

"Maybe we should let 'im smell it again," Henry suggested, so he put the handkerchief back up under Huck's snout.

"Go git 'im, boy," I commanded.

And Huck continued with his sniffing, leading us around the pond again, but this time when we passed a waterway on the far side of the swamp leading west, Huck scratched the wooden seat of the boat and stuck his head in the direction of that waterway.

"He's tellin' us to go through that channel," I said excitedly.

"Hallelujah, Huck!" Henry exclaimed. "Good boy!"

So, we just kept following Huck's directions and paying attention to every which way he wanted us to go. We wound in and out of little waterways and ducked under and in between branches. Sometimes he'd lead us one way, only to make us turn around and head a different direction altogether. After more than an hour, we were way over by Suwannee Creek near Cravens Hammock, and I wasn't so sure Huck was really leading us anywhere in particular. What I *was* sure of was that if Grandma knew how far we were from Honey Island, she would certainly be using her scolding voice with us when we got home.

"Henry, maybe ya should start prayin' again," I said as I sat down on the middle seat of the boat to rest my legs.

Henry leaned over the side of the boat, swirled a gator hole, and slurped a big drink of water. Then he made one for Huck, who leaned over and lapped up a drink too.

"Lord, ya already know what kind of predicament we're in," Henry began praying as he wiped his hand across his mouth to catch the extra drips of water. "Please give us a sign."

I leaned over, swirled a whirlpool with my hand, and sucked up some cool swamp water and let it trickle down my throat. Then I splashed some water on my face, and as I lifted my head, I saw something between the trees over in the distance.

"Henry!" I whispered, standing up and squinting in the hot sun to get a better look. "Henry! I think there's a lean-to over there on that little island."

"Hallelujah, it's a sign!" Henry said a little bit too loud.

"Shh!" I said. "There might be somebody in there."

My heart beat hard inside my chest. Maybe Huck really had led us right to the bandits and the somebody in there was the real hog bandits. This really would be a perfect place for the bandits to hide out. After they stole the hogs, they could've hidden them at Hollow Log Pond. Later, they could've moved the hogs over here to this lean-to. Then, when the bandits were ready, they could take the hogs down Suwannee Creek to the river and finally out of the Okefenokee. And once they were out, it would be easy to go into Williamsburg or Fargo and sell the hogs without anyone ever knowing where the hogs came from.

Huck scratched at the seat, wanting us to move forward again straight for where the lean-to was. Now that we were here and might have found the hog bandits for real, I wasn't exactly sure what to do next.

Thankfully, Henry must've sensed my uncertainty because he already had his eyes closed and was rocking back and forth in prayer.

I moved the boat a little closer to the island to get a better look so that I could see if there was any activity, but I didn't see any movement. I knew the only way to get to the lean-to was by boat, so I scanned the swamp's edge looking for a boat lying in the bushes somewhere. The closer we got to the island, the more convinced I was that there wasn't anyone in that lean-to because there wasn't a boat anywhere in sight.

"The bandits are probably off doin' some low-down, no-good thing," I whispered to Henry. "All we have t'do is wait for 'em to come back."

"Oh, Lord, have mercy, Elsie Mae," Henry wailed, opening his eyes. "Do ya really think that's a good idea?"

"'Course I do," I said. "We're goin' to hide in those bushes over there," I explained, pointing.

And as I pushed us toward the bushes, so we could crouch underneath them and wait, my stomach flip-flopped back and forth between being excited about being a hero and scared to death that I wouldn't be a big enough one to keep from losing Huck.

Chapter 27

After hiding in the bushes for a long time, Huck was asleep, Henry had just about worn out the words of Psalm 23 by reciting them over and over, and I was so cramped I thought I'd never be able to stand up straight again. The thick branches shaded us from the hot sun, but even so, kneeling on the bottom of the boat and crouching down the way we were, I was beginning to think I didn't have what it took to be a hero.

Just as Henry finished reciting Psalm 23 for at least the millionth time, Huck picked up his head, and a few seconds later, I heard voices. They were faraway at first, but soon I was able to understand parts of their conversation.

"I say we stay here one more night. That's it!" one of them said.

"What?" the other exclaimed. "And walk away from this gold mine?"

Huck sniffed the air, but I scratched his head to keep him from standing up.

"We're gonna git caught one of these days."

"Yer always thinkin' about gittin' caught. Shut up already and stop worryin' so much."

Henry and I looked at each other. Our faces were so close together as we hunched down in the bottom of the boat that I wondered if Henry could hear and feel my heart pounding.

"Nice of those ol' moonshine boys to take the blame fer us fer a few days, wadn't it?"

I saw Henry's eyes widen, and it was like I was looking in the mirror because I knew my eyes had to be doing the exact same thing. These really were the hog bandits!

Both men laughed until they were coughing and spitting. Their voices were much louder now, but I still couldn't see them from where we were hiding. I tried to steady my breath as we listened to see what they would do next.

"All I wanna do right now is get me some shut-eye," one of the men said.

"You and me both."

"Yeah, the hogs'll be happy we're takin' a night off."

This set the men laughing again.

When they got close enough to the island, I could finally see their boat. I kept scratching Huck's head to keep him from getting up, and Henry and I watched the two men as they got out on the island and stumbled around. Finally, they dragged their boat up onto the small clearing. Then they reached back into the boat and each grabbed a big jug and took a drink. That explained the laughing and the stumbling. Then they headed up the small hill toward the lean-to singing, "'Way down upon the Suwannee River…'"

When the two men were out of sight, I waited a minute longer to be sure they were all the way inside their lean-to. Then I pushed our boat out from under the bushes where we had been hiding.

Once out in the open, I breathed in a big gulp of fresh air. Huck stood up on the seat, put his snout in the air, and sniffed. Henry looked at me and whispered, "What're we gonna do now?"

I quietly picked up the pole and pushed our boat toward the island, being sure I didn't make any splashing sounds with the pole.

"We're goin' t'do the only thing we can do," I said, keeping my voice low. "Take their boat."

"What?" Henry said. "That's stealin'."

"Shh," I whispered. "It's the only way to stop *them* from stealin'."

"Lord, have mercy," Henry mumbled as our boat slid up onto the clearing next to where the hog bandits' boat was hiding.

"The faster we do this, the better," I whispered.

"Do ya really think this is a good idea?" Henry hissed.

Before I could answer, Huck jumped out of the boat and started sniffing and dancing as he followed the invisible path of the bandits.

"Henry!" I whispered. "Git Huck!"

I held our boat in place with the pole as Henry jumped out of the boat after Huck.

"C'mon, boy," Henry whispered, patting his legs.

Huck wanted to keep going toward the lean-to, but by some miracle, maybe because of all of Henry's praying, Huck turned around, listened to Henry, and followed him back to the boat.

"Go grab their boat and tie it to ours," I whispered to Henry as I reached out to get hold of Huck.

"Oh no!" Henry said. "I'm not goin' to be the one t'do that."

"Oh, good gracious, Henry," I snapped. "Jus' git in and hold this pole then, and whatever ya do, *don't* let go of Huck."

Henry climbed back in the boat, dragging Huck with him. Then he grabbed the pole from me with one hand to keep the boat in place and kept holding Huck with the other. I jumped up on the shore and pulled the hog bandits' boat back into the water carefully so as not to make a sound.

Uncle Owen always kept a rope in the boat for tying up his dogs if he ever needed to, so I used that rope to attach the front of the hog bandits' boat to the back of ours.

"OK," I whispered, stepping back into our boat. "Let's go!"

"Lord, fergive us," Henry mumbled.

He handed the pole back to me but still held on to Huck as he sat down on the front seat.

As we pulled away from the island, we heard a loud sound coming from the lean-to. It was the hog bandits, and they were snoring. All that moonshine they'd been drinking was a real blessing. It would give us time to get back to Honey Island to tell everyone we'd found the real hog bandits before those two low-downs even woke up. Just another answer to Henry's prayers.

Soon we'd be the heroes I always dreamed we'd be, but none of that mattered if it wasn't enough to keep me from losing Huck.

Chapter 28

"Grandpa! Grandpa!" I yelled as Henry and I ran up the trail toward the house.

Huck loped after us, not knowing how much of a hero he was about to become.

"What 'r' ya kids yellin' 'bout?" Grandma asked from the porch where she sat in the rocking chair snapping beans.

"It's the hog bandits," I said, out of breath as we ran up the steps. "We found 'em! Fer real this time! Where's Grandpa? Is he back from Hamp's yet?"

Grandma's bowl of snap beans clattered to the porch floor as she stood up to hold me by the shoulders. "Elsie Mae, what've y'all been up to?"

"We found 'em, Grandma!" I exclaimed. "But we gotta hurry, or they'll git away. Where's Grandpa?"

"Child, ya better slow down and tell me what's goin' on," Grandma said.

Just then, Grandpa came around the side of the house, wiping his forehead with the rag he always kept in his pocket.

"What's all the yellin' 'bout out here?" he asked.

I pulled myself away from Grandma and jumped back down the porch steps to where Grandpa was standing at the corner of the house.

"We found 'em, Grandpa! The hog bandits," I said. "And it was Huck who led us right to 'em."

I reached down and scratched Huck on the head as he stood next to me almost as if he was waiting on me to tell Grandpa what a great job he'd done.

"What're ya talkin' 'bout, Elsie Mae?" Grandpa asked.

"The hog bandits are over by Cravens Hammock in a lean-to on a little island," I explained. "But we gotta hurry cuz they could wake up and git away! So c'mon!"

I started walking toward the trail that led to the landing, hoping I'd told enough of the story to get Grandpa to follow me.

"Elsie Mae, yer gonna have to slow down and tell me what's goin' on," Grandpa said, putting his hands on his hips.

"Well, ya see, Uncle Zeke," Henry explained. "We

done somethin' we shouldn't of, but we done it fer a real good reason."

Why did Henry always have to bring up the sinful side of everything?

I turned back around to face Grandpa.

"OK, here's what happened," I said, and then I explained the whole story.

I eventually told Grandpa about the boat that we stole, but not before I told him all the other good stuff we'd done. As I talked, Grandma came down into the yard from the porch and interrupted my story with more gasps and "Oh my's!" than I could count.

Once I finished, Grandpa said, "Well, then we better git on over there right quick."

Then he hollered, "Owen! Lone! Let's go!"

The two of them must've been out back by the barn helping Grandpa with something, because in less than a minute we saw them coming around the corner of the house. As soon as we saw them, Huck stuck his nose in the air, and then the next thing I knew his snout was on the ground sniffing a path leading right up toward Uncle Lone. Once he got up close enough, he jumped up on Uncle Lone and started licking him half to death. Henry and I looked at each other, and I got a real strange feeling in my stomach.

"Git this gol'darn dog offa me!" Uncle Lone yelled.

I ran after Huck and pulled him down off Uncle Lone.

"That animal's a menace," Uncle Lone said, brushing himself off.

"Never bothers me," Uncle Owen said. "He must jus' like the taste of ornery."

And Uncle Owen laughed at his own joke, but Henry and I didn't laugh. Having Huck jump up on Uncle Lone after Huck had just been tracking the hog bandits might mean that Uncle Lone was more than just ornery.

"Boys," Grandpa said to Uncle Owen and Uncle Lone, "'nough of that shim-shackin' 'round. Elsie and Henry jus' found the hog bandits, and they's passed out in a lean-to over by Cravens Hammock. We need to git there quick so's we can capture 'em before they wake up."

"Are ya kiddin' with me?" Uncle Owen said. "How did the two of ya track down those scrapers?"

Uncle Lone didn't say anything. He just scratched his forehead and rubbed his hands together.

"We don't have time to explain the story now," Grandpa said. "They'll tell ya on the way."

"Oh no they won't," Grandma said. "Those two young'uns are stayin' right here with me."

I groaned. Now that it was time for the capture of the hog bandits, Henry and I weren't even going to get to go?

"Sarah," Grandpa said firmly. "They's the ones who found the bandits. They's the ones who're gonna bring 'em in."

"Well, I ain't goin'," Uncle Lone said, sounding agitated. "I got other stuff t'do."

"After all that braggin' 'bout bringin' these scoundrels to justice, and yer not even gonna go 'long?" Grandma asked.

"He's jus' jealous that Elsie and Henry found those doggoned hog bandits when he's been searchin' one end of the swamp to the other lookin' for 'em," Uncle Owen said, laughing to himself.

"Don't matter to me why he ain't goin'," Grandpa said. "We jus' ain't got time to waste standin' 'round here talkin'. Owen, grab our rifles and some rope from 'round back, and let's go!"

But in as much of a hurry as Grandpa was to leave, Uncle Lone disappeared around the back of the house before we'd even headed down the trail toward the boat.

Nobody but Henry and I knew that Uncle Lone could be more than just mad that Henry and I had been the ones to find the hog bandits. It might could be *a lot* more than that, but there was no time for that now. The hog bandits were waiting.

Chapter 29

When we reached Cravens Hammock, I pointed out the island where the bandits were hiding.

"We can pull the boat up onto the clearin' there," I said. "Their lean-to is up that little hill behind those bushes."

I felt important being the one giving the instructions, and Huck sat by my side like a deputy sheriff. I hoped with all my heart that his success in finding these bandits would make the real sheriff change his mind about making Huck go back up to Pierce County.

"All right," Grandpa said, "we better be careful now. These two low-downs most likely got guns. We don't want to git into a standoff with 'em."

"The Lord is my shepherd," Henry whispered as he began rocking back and forth.

Up until Grandpa mentioned the guns, Henry had seemed pretty calm, but now he was back to his usual praying self.

"Don't matter if they has guns," Uncle Owen said. "If they're sleepin' off their moonshine, they won't be any match fer the two of us."

"Jus' take it easy, Owen," Grandpa said. "We don't want anything gittin' outta hand here. Let's be as peaceful as possible, 'specially when we got these young'uns with us."

"I think Uncle Owen's right. I don't think we have to worry," I said. "They was 'bout as drunk as could be when they stumbled up the hill. Plus, we got Henry prayin' over there."

I nodded to Henry, who sat in the back of the boat with his eyes closed, rocking the boat gently with his prayers.

As we got closer to the island, Huck started pacing nervously in the boat.

"What's the matter with 'im," Uncle Owen asked.

"He can smell the bandits and wants to pick up their trail again," I explained. "Easy, boy," I said, scratching Huck's head.

"OK," Grandpa said. "When we git up to the clearin', you and Henry and Huck stay here in the boat. Owen and I will go up to the lean-to and try to catch those scoundrels off guard."

The boat slid onto the clearing of the island, and Grandpa and Uncle Owen got out, each with their rifles and some rope slung over their shoulders. Huck wiggled and scratched and danced around. It was all I could do to keep him in the boat.

Henry just kept rocking and praying.

"Easy, boy," I said. "Stay here."

As I held on to Huck's neck, I watched Grandpa and Uncle Owen cautiously make their way up the hill toward the lean-to. We still hadn't heard a sound out of the bandits. Once Grandpa and Uncle Owen got up the hill and around the bushes, I couldn't see them anymore.

I strained to hear sounds that might give me a clue about what was going on, and then it started. It sounded like it does when a coon gets loose in the chicken yard. Lots of flapping and fluttering, lots of screaming and squawking. Huck scratched his claws into the bottom of the boat like he wanted to dig his way to the deepest part of the swamp.

Then I saw them coming down the hill. Grandpa first, holding the arm of one of the bandits, and Uncle Owen next, dragging the second one by the suspender strap. Both bandits had their hands tied behind their backs. As soon as Huck saw them, he broke free from me and barreled up the hill straight at the bandits.

He jumped up in their faces and licked them, and he even knocked one of them down to the ground.

"He's killin' me! He's killin' me!" yelled the one on the ground, turning away from Huck's tongue. He looked to be just about drowning in Huck's drool.

"Git that animal away from me!" the other one screamed.

Huck roughed those guys up worse than any of us ever could. He wasn't trying to hurt them—he was just being his usual friendly self—but those bandits didn't know what hit them.

"Hallelujah!" Henry exclaimed once he opened his eyes and saw what was going on.

And Grandpa, Uncle Owen, Henry, and I laughed and laughed. It was the funniest thing we'd ever seen and the most satisfying too.

Chapter 30

Later that day was almost a repeat of the day the moonshine boys had been caught. The real hog bandits, with their wrists tied behind their backs, sat on the big stump in the yard, but this time our captives were propped up against each other because they were still sleeping off their moonshine.

Grandpa and Uncle Owen stood in the chinaberry trees' shade talking. Henry and I sat on the porch swing, gliding back and forth with Huck sleeping at our feet, and Grandma sat in one of the rocking chairs snapping more of her beans.

As I rocked the porch swing, my worried heart prayed silently that my plan of catching the hog bandits to save Huck was divine providence. I knew I wasn't as holy as Henry James, but I sure hoped God wouldn't hold that against me when something as important as keeping Huck was at stake.

It wasn't long before we heard *"Yowwweeeee! Yowwweeeee!"* coming up from the water. It was Hamp. He had gone off to fetch Sheriff Jones once he'd heard about us catching the real bandits.

Hamp's swamp call pierced my prayers and filled me with dread. Now that Sheriff Jones was here, my doubts wrestled my hope to the ground, and I worried that my plan to save Huck had been a big, huge mistake. Even so, I jumped off the swing with Henry and headed down the porch steps to wait in the yard with Grandpa and Uncle Owen. Huck loped out into the yard behind us. Soon Hamp came walking up the trail from the landing with Sheriff Jones following right behind him.

"Howdy, y'all," Sheriff Jones said when he got close.

And he tipped his hat to all of us.

"Well, we know we got 'em this time," Grandpa said, pointing to the stump where the two men sat slumped against each other, still sleeping.

"I heard it was that dog that led the young'uns right to these scoundrels," Sheriff Jones said, looking right at Grandpa.

As soon as the sheriff said that, I realized how foolish it was for me to think that having Huck help us find the hog bandits would be the sure way for me to keep him. My stomach scrunched up with worry as I held my breath hoping that, by some miracle, the sheriff wouldn't see Huck's help as a reason to take him away. Everyone in the yard was quiet, and I knew everyone was thinking the same thing.

"That dog's obviously been trained well if he found those two scrapers like he did," Sheriff Jones said. "I really should let everyone upstate know that the trackin' dog they lost months ago is alive and well and livin' right here in the swamp."

I felt my skin go cold and clammy, the same way it had in the damp, dark danger of Hollow Log Pond that very first day Henry and I had been there together when the hog bandits shot at us. My heart pounded, and the ringing in my ears sounded louder than Uncle Owen's swamp call.

Out of the corner of my eye, I saw Henry James's lips whispering prayers, and I noticed Grandpa's face turn to stone. His expression made it easy for me to see where Uncle Lone got his orneriness.

"Now wait a minute!" Grandpa said, breaking the silence and cutting into the fear that was pounding and ringing in my head.

"That dog was a stray runnin' 'round *our* swamp, and if it wasn't fer Elsie Mae here, he probly wouldn't even be alive!" Grandpa said, sounding madder than I'd ever heard him sound.

Trickles of silent tears slipped down my face as I knelt by Huck, who stood next to me. I felt Grandma's hand touch my head.

"Yep," Sheriff Jones said, "and that's why if anyone come down here from Pierce County tryin' to take that dog away from Elsie Mae, they're gonna have to wrestle me first before they wrestle you."

We all exhaled in relief.

No one said anything.

What could we say?

Sheriff Jones wasn't going to let anyone take Huck away!

Now my silent tears turned to sobs, and I buried my head in the folds of Huck's neck. Grandma's hand rested on my head, anointing me with relief.

"Hallelujah and amen!" Henry James finally shouted, shattering the surprised and relief-filled silence.

And everyone laughed out loud, letting go of the worry we'd all been holding on to.

"Well, I best be gitting these two over to the cell that's waitin' fer 'em at Traders Hill," Sheriff Jones said.

"We'd be much obliged," Grandpa said.

I looked up from Huck with happy tears smeared all

over my face to see Grandpa reach out to shake the sheriff's hand. His face of stone had been transformed by Sheriff Jones's kindness back into his usual expression of friendly good cheer.

The sheriff walked over, shook the hog bandits awake, and grabbed them by the arms.

"Yer hog bandit days is over, boys," Sheriff Jones said as he stood them up and dragged them across the yard toward the gate.

In their dazed stupor, they didn't even fight back, but even so, Hamp followed the sheriff and the bandits through the gate, so he could go along on the trip to Traders Hill.

"Y'all have a good day now," Sheriff Jones called over his shoulder as he disappeared down the trail leading to the water.

"We sure will!" Grandma called after him.

I was too happy to speak. I laid my cheek on Huck's head. I wasn't just planning on having a good day. I was planning on having a good rest of the summer. Huck was safe, and from the news Hamp had told us about the ship canal, the swamp was safe too. On top of that, Henry, Huck, and I were the big heroes in the hog bandit mystery. Having a good rest of the summer was going to be as easy as huckleberry pie.

Chapter 31

The next day, Henry, Huck, and I sat in Uncle Owen's boat on the edge of Billys Lake right near the spot where Henry had baptized me.

"Uncle Zeke and Aunt Sarah aren't going to let us go all the way to Traders Hill by ourselves," Henry James said. "'Sides, the president's already stopped that ship company, so ya don't have to worry 'bout him payin' attention to yer letter no more."

"I know," I said, "but it's jus' that I really had my heart set on gittin' our picture in the newspaper fer findin' those hog bandits."

Grandma had sent Henry and me out to catch some catfish for dinner. She planned to make another heroes' feast for us, and it's not that I wasn't looking forward to it, it was just that I kept thinking how exciting it would be to have the whole county know what a big hero I was. It might be the best chance I ever had to make everyone say, "That Elsie Mae is really somethin'!"

I knew there was still a possibility that when the president came out with his plan to save the swamp, he'd mention my letter. But what if my letter didn't really have anything to do with him saving the swamp? Or even if it did, what if the president forgot all about mentioning me? Getting in the newspaper for saving the hogs from the hog bandits was a sure thing, and I didn't want to waste that chance. So, since no one seemed to be talking about making Henry and me into some kind of headline, I thought maybe it would be a good idea for the two of us to head over to Traders Hill ourselves and pay a little visit to the *Charlton County Caller* to see what we could do about that. But Henry wasn't seeing it that way.

"Elsie Mae," he said, "first, ya tol' me ya wanted to find the hog bandits cuz it was the right thing t'do. Then, ya said it was all about gittin' in the newspaper so ya could git the president's attention and git him to stop that ship canal. And next, ya said we had to find the hog bandits to save Huck. But now I'm startin' to wonder if it was always 'bout somethin' else."

"Like what?" I said, feeling myself getting annoyed with Henry.

"Yer pride," Henry said.

222

"Pride shmide, Henry James!" I exclaimed. "It's only right that we should git the recognition we deserve. What good is doin' somethin' great if ya don't get any glory?"

"I knew it!" Henry James said matter-a-factly, "It *is* yer pride talkin'."

"Ya better believe it's my pride talkin'!" I said, getting more than annoyed, "I'm proud of what we done, and I have every right to be!"

"Oh, Elsie," Henry said in his preacher voice, sounding like he felt sorry for me. "Ya know what the Lord says. Pride goes before the fall."

"Oh, Henry," I snapped. "Don't pretend like ya don't like all this attention we been gittin'. First, fer rescuin' that piglet and then fer findin' the real hog bandits."

"Enjoyin' the attention God gives ya and thankin' him fer it ain't the same as disobeyin' Uncle Zeke and Aunt Sarah to go all the way to Traders Hill jus' so ya can git even *more* attention," Henry James said, sounding like a Sunday school teacher scolding me.

How was it that Henry always found a way to make himself sound better than me?

I pulled up my fishing line and threw it harder than needed to a spot a little farther from the swamp's edge.

"Well, *you* should be thankin' God fer *me* because if it wasn't fer me, you wouldn't be gittin' any kind of glory at all," I said.

I hated how mean I sounded. It reminded me of the way my older sisters sometimes talked when they were being especially nasty to me.

"Jus' remember, Elsie," Henry said. "Earthly glory is fleeting, but the Lord says a humble heart is eternal."

"Jus' remember, Henry," I said. "Better to git rid of the plank in yer own eye before removin' the speck of sawdust in yer neighbor's."

His surprised expression proved that I knew a lot more scripture than he'd ever imagined I did.

But then Henry said, "Elsie Mae, yer startin' to sound as ornery and boastful as Uncle Lone."

That's when I wished Henry really did have a plank in his eye so that I could take it out myself and hit him over the head with it.

Chapter 32

By the time we got back from Billys Lake, slid up onto the landing at Honey Island, and got out of Uncle Owen's boat, I wasn't even speaking to Henry. Grandma wondered why our mess of catfish was so meager. Maybe it had something to do with the fact that Henry and I had spent most of the morning arguing. I was tired of him always finding fault with what I did. I could've stayed back home if I wanted that.

But the real problem was that deep down, I knew Henry was right. I *was* just being prideful. I really should have just been thankful for how everything had turned out.

The ship canal was being stopped, and the swamp was safe. Henry and I really *were* the hog bandit heroes. And most importantly, Huck was all mine.

But as I sat on the porch, already smelling the fish

frying, I just couldn't help but think about how being a hero didn't quite feel the way I'd always imagined it would. I creaked the porch swing back and forth slowly to match my melancholy mood.

"There she is!"

I looked up to see Uncle Owen walking through the gate, and alongside him was a man I'd never seen before. I could tell by the man's clean, pressed pants and his collared shirt that he wasn't from around here.

"Hi, Uncle Owen!" I said, standing up and walking toward the porch steps.

"Harper," Uncle Owen said as the two of them continued to walk toward the house, "I'd like ya to meet my niece, Elsie Mae. She's the brains behind the capture of those hog bandits."

"Well, it's nice to meet you," the man said, holding out his hand to shake mine as he and Uncle Owen came up the steps.

I had never shaken an adult's hand before, but I reached out and shook hands with Harper like I'd been doing it my whole life.

"Nice to meet ya, sir," I said.

"Elsie," Uncle Owen said, "Mr. Harper here jus' moved to Traders Hill from up north a ways, and jus' got a job as a reporter for the *Charlton County Caller*. I ran into him up at the Hill this mornin' when I went in to sell some syrup. A few folks in the store got to talkin' 'bout what you and Henry James done, findin' those hog bandits and all, and Harper seemed real interested. So he decided he'd come 'long home with me to meet the two of ya so he might could do a li'l article 'bout the whole hog bandit mystery. What do ya think 'bout that?"

"Hallelujah!" I said, feeling myself fill up with pride. "Will ya be takin' any pictures, Mr. Harper?" I asked, crossing my fingers.

"You betcha," Harper said, holding up the camera that hung from a strap under his arm.

How about that? I wasn't even going to have to leave Honey Island in order to get my picture in the newspaper.

"Folks love to see what real heroes look like," Harper said, smiling.

"Real heroes. That's a real joke."

We all turned to see Uncle Lone standing in the yard on the side of the house. He must've heard Uncle Owen explain what Harper was here to do. I guess I could understand why he wouldn't be happy about it.

"That's my brother, Lone," Uncle Owen said. "He had his heart set on findin' those hog bandits, but the young'uns beat 'im to it."

"They ain't beat me to nothin'," Uncle Lone mumbled.

"Nice to meet you, Lone," Harper said, holding out his hand to shake Uncle Lone's, even though Uncle Lone was still way over at the corner of the house.

Uncle Lone turned and walked back in the direction he'd come from.

"Lone, where ya goin'?" Uncle Owen called after him. "Ma's probly got dinner real soon."

"I got stuff t'do," Uncle Lone grumped, and then he was out of sight behind the house.

"Well," Uncle Owen said, "jus' more fer all of us, I guess. Elsie, where's Grandpa and Henry?"

"Probly 'round back in the barn, sir," I said.

"Well, tell 'em we got company," Uncle Owen said, "And bring 'em 'round to the porch. Harper can ask you and Henry some questions while Ma finishes up cookin' what's already smellin' mighty delicious."

Uncle Owen and Harper sat down in the rocking chairs on the porch, and I jumped down the steps and took off around back toward the garden. I couldn't believe it! Henry and I were going to be in the *Charlton County Caller*. Maybe being a hero really was going to feel as good as I'd always imagined it would.

Chapter 33

Ma'am," Harper said licking his fingers one at a time, "I have to say that's the best darn cornbread I think I've ever tasted. Truth is, everything I ate was the best I've ever tasted. I never knew food could taste so good."

Everyone laughed, and I think Grandma blushed a little.

"Jus' wait till ya taste the huckleberry pie we have fer dessert," I said happily.

"It might be a sin to say, Mr. Harper..." Henry James spoke up. "But Aunt Sarah's pie is the best thing this side of the pearly gates."

Everyone laughed again even harder.

Grandma wiped her forehead with her dish towel, trying to hide her bright-red face.

"Henry's right, Mr. Harper. It's the best of the best," I said. "Fact is, it's so good that Huck's even named after it."

"Is that right?" Harper said, smiling. "Well, if my hands weren't so full of all this wonderful food, I'd write that in my notes and add it to my story."

Before we'd all come in to eat dinner, Harper had sat with Henry James and me on the porch and listened to us tell him all about our adventures with the hog bandits. He hung on every word we said as his hand flew across the white pages of his notebook, recording just about every single thing we said. And I didn't care what Henry James said about pride coming before the fall because I could tell Henry was feeling pretty darn proud that people in Charlton County were going to be reading all about the two of us.

The very best part came when Harper sat Henry and me on the porch swing with Huck at our feet and took our picture.

Once we all came inside to eat, Harper had put his notebook away, and I was pretty sure he was all done taking notes for his story. But I wasn't quite finished with everything *I* wanted to tell him. Now that he'd mentioned the story again, I thought it might be the perfect time for me to tell him about one more important thing—my letter to the president. If he made mention of that in his story, everyone would not only know that I had saved the swampers from the hog bandits, but also that it was likely I was the one who saved the entire Okefenokee Swamp from being ruined by that ship canal.

But before I had a chance to give Harper a reason to take out his notebook again, we all heard, "*Yeeooooow! Yeeoooooow!*"

"What's Farley doin' up here?" Grandpa said, looking at Uncle Owen. "You two ain't plannin' on goin' huntin' later t'day, are ya?"

"Not that I remember," Uncle Owen said.

"You mean to tell me that you know who that is from hearing that sound?" Harper asked with a look of amazement all over his face.

"Why sure," Grandpa said. "Farley's been usin' the same swamp call since he was a li'l bitty thing."

Harper wiped his hands on his clean, pressed pants and reached down to take his notebook out of the cloth bag that lay at his feet. He grabbed the pencil he had resting behind his ear, flipped open his notebook, and scratched his pencil over the blank page as fast as could be.

"We best go see what's brought 'im up this way," Grandpa said.

We all pushed out from under the table and followed

Grandpa out to the porch. Even before we all got out there, Farley came panting up the trail.

"Is Lone here?" he asked, out of breath.

"I suppose he's back over at our cabin," Uncle Owen said. "Why?"

"What's wrong, son?" Grandpa asked.

"It's Sheriff Jones," Farley said, trying hard to catch his breath. "He's comin' for Lone. Says he's mixed up with those hog bandits."

"What?" Grandma exclaimed. "Lord, have mercy!"

Henry and I looked at each other, and I could tell from the look on Henry's face that just like me, he wasn't all that surprised. In fact, hearing this news about Uncle Lone made a whole lot of sense.

"Son," Grandpa said. "Yer gonna have to explain yerself some."

And when Grandpa said that, Harper flipped to a fresh new page in his notebook and hovered his pencil over the page, just waiting for Farley to start spilling the details.

"Seems Lone had a whole plan cooked up with those two low-downs," Farley explained.

"What?" Uncle Owen asked. "How'd he ever git mixed up with 'em?"

232

"I guess he met 'em over at Traders Hill a while back when he was up there sellin' his syrup. They got to talkin' and turns out they're cousins of one of the fellas Lone spent time with at Folkston Prison. Well, one thing led to 'nother, and 'fore ya know it, the three of 'em were hatchin' a plan."

Farley took a deep breath and went on. "The two scoundrels was gonna steal a coupla hogs, wait till a reward was offered, and then make like Lone was the one who caught 'em in the act. After Lone turned 'em in, and they got locked up, Lone was gonna somehow help 'em escape, and then they was all gonna split the reward."

Harper's pencil was flying over his notebook page faster than a mosquito toward the light.

"So what happened to their plan?" Grandpa asked.

"Well, when the two scrapers heard the reward was only fifty dollars, they didn't think splittin' that three ways was nearly 'nough fer all their trouble. So, Lone told 'em he wouldn't even take any of the reward money, and the two of 'em could split it with each other."

"Why would he do that?" Uncle Owen asked.

"He tol' 'em the money wasn't important to him. All he really cared about was being a hero."

I felt an uncomfortable twinge in my stomach when Farley said that.

"But the real problem came when the bandits found out that they could actually make a lot more money stealin' hogs than collectin' some measly reward, so they tol' Lone the deal was off."

Farley continued, "And once those two low-downs decided to keep on stealin' hogs, they told Lone if he ever squealed on 'em, they'd start stealin' yer hogs too."

"That's why none of our hogs come up missin'," Henry said.

"Lord, have mercy!" Grandma said again. "What are we gonna do 'bout this?"

"Well, that's what I come fer, ma'am," Farley said. "Sheriff Jones tol' my pa that if Lone turns 'imself in, he might git a lighter sentence, so Pa sent me over to git Lone to Camp Cornelia by t'night so that we can git 'im over to Traders Hill first thing in the mornin' to turn 'imself in."

"Owen," Grandpa said sternly, "go git yer brother."

And a short time later, Grandma was cryin', and Grandpa was headin' off in Farley's boat with Farley, Uncle Lone, Uncle Owen, and Harper, who hadn't stopped writing in his notebook since Farley's swamp call. Funny how when

Harper was writing about Henry and me, I had loved the sound of his pencil scratching up his blank pages, but now that he was writing about Uncle Lone, it felt like that scratching sound was on the inside of my head. I wished I could take that pencil of his and crack it right in two.

Farley's boat slipped behind the branches as he guided it away from the island. As I watched it disappear, I thought about how Uncle Lone was probably going to get his picture in the newspaper after all, but it wasn't going to be for being a hero.

Henry and I walked Grandma back up to the house and sat her in her rocking chair. Henry got her Bible from the shelf by her bed, opened to the page that wasn't attached anymore, the one that stuck out farther than all the other pages, and even though he knew it by heart, he read Grandma her favorite passage out of her beloved Bible. And while I sat listening to the words of Psalm 23, which Henry James would surely wear out in his lifetime, I stared at the uneaten huckleberry pie that sat up on the shelf next to the sink. Not getting to eat that pie was surely a sign that being a hero would never ever be as good as what I'd imagined it to be.

Chapter 34

The next afternoon, Henry James and I sat on the porch swing with Huck lying at our feet. The muggy day clung to us like moss hanging from a tree. A light rain pattered against the leaves of the trees near the house, but it didn't bring any relief from the heat.

"Maybe we should sing a hymn to cheer us up," Henry James finally said.

"Henry, there ain't no hymn that's gonna fix the mess Uncle Lone's got 'imself into," I said.

I had gone to bed the night before thinking about how having Harper around when we found out about Uncle Lone only made things worse, and Harper had been up to the house to do a story about Henry James and me. Because of that, I felt kind of responsible for all that worseness, so I surely didn't feel much like singing.

Even though Uncle Lone could really be mean sometimes, it seemed awful unfair that he'd gotten himself into so much trouble when all he was trying to do was be a hero.

I had woken up that morning to the sound of Grandma creaking back and forth in her rocking chair, and she and the chair and the creaking hadn't stopped once since I'd climbed down the loft ladder. Henry and I had eaten leftover cornbread for breakfast and again at noon, while Grandma stared off into the distance not saying a word. We hoped Grandpa and Uncle Owen would know what to do to get Grandma to stop staring and rocking, but they hadn't come back yet.

"How long ya think till Uncle Zeke gits back?" Henry James asked.

"Not sure," I said. "I hope soon."

And it was as if us mentioning them for about the hundredth time made them appear, because I looked up to see them walking through the gate and into the yard. Their rain-wet clothes clung to them, making them look as dreary as we all were feeling.

"Yer back!" I exclaimed, standing up quickly and heading down the porch steps.

Henry followed me out into the yard, even though it was still raining.

237

"That we are," Uncle Owen said. "It was a long night and an even longer mornin'."

"Is Uncle Lone in jail?" I asked.

"That he is," Grandpa said with a pained look on his face.

"Lord, help us," Henry James whispered.

"Amen to that, son," Grandpa said, ruffling Henry James's hair. "We'll be needin' all the help we can git. Even with turnin' himself in, Lone could be facin' quite a lengthy li'l stay in Folkston this time 'round."

"Really?" I asked.

The rain sprinkles, which had been a cool relief when we stepped off the porch, now dampened my clothes and my mood, which I had thought was already as damp as it could get.

"'Fraid so," Grandpa said. "But we're jus' gonna have to git through it somehow. Now where's Sarah, and how's she doin'?"

Henry and I looked at each other. Neither of us wanted to be the one to tell Grandpa that she hadn't gotten out of her rocking chair all day.

"She's restin' inside," I said.

It wasn't really the truth, but it wasn't quite a lie either.

"I'll go fill her in on what happened this mornin'," Grandpa said, heading for the house.

"I'm goin' back home to catch some shut-eye, Pa," Uncle Owen said. "Tell Ma I'll be back up fer supper."

"All right, Son," Grandpa said over his shoulder as he walked toward the house.

Uncle Owen waited until Grandpa was almost inside before he said, "Henry James, I've got a bit of a silver linin' fer ya in this mess of a time we're havin'."

"What do ya mean?" Henry asked.

"Well, this dark cloud we've got over us at the moment has a tiny ray of light shinin' through it," Uncle Owen said.

Henry and I looked at Uncle Owen in confusion.

"How would ya like yer own dog fer a bit?" Uncle Owen asked.

"A dog!" Henry James exclaimed.

"Yeah," Uncle Owen said. "I was thinkin' that since Lone's gonna be gone fer a while, ya might want to take care of Dog fer 'im. I've got my own four dogs to keep track of, and I sure don't need 'nother one."

"Really?"

Henry James was smiling bigger than I thought a person could smile, and I understood why. I remembered how happy I was the day I got Huck.

"I'll bring 'im with me when I come back up here fer

supper t'night," Uncle Owen said, and then he headed off around the house on his way to his own cabin.

"I'm sure sorry to hear 'bout Uncle Lone being in jail," Henry said, trying to push down his happiness some.

"Henry, feelin' happy about Dog don't mean yer not sad 'bout Uncle Lone," I said.

"I know," Henry James said. "I jus' don't want to be the kinda person who takes pleasure in someone else's misery, that's all."

"Henry," I said, "you could never be that kinda person even if ya tried."

I looked down at my overalls that were now more wet than dry.

"Do ya want to go out in the boat fer a while?" I asked Henry.

"Do ya think we should?" he asked.

"Why are ya askin'?" I said. "Because it's rainin', or because ya think we should be mournin' 'bout Uncle Lone?"

"I don't know. I jus'…"

"We can't sit 'round on the porch all day," I said. "C'mon, Huck," I called.

So, Henry and Huck followed me down to the landing, and we headed out in the boat going nowhere in particular.

The rain was barely a sprinkle now, but I liked how the grayness of the sky and the misty air made everything look eerie. I poled the boat, cutting it through the calm, smooth water that was polka-dotted with smaller-than-raindrop sprinkles. Huck lay sleeping in his usual spot, and Henry and I didn't speak, letting the rainy sounds of the swamp be our only conversation. But then I noticed a piece of paper tacked up to a tree along the edge of the waterway we traveled.

"Hey, Henry," I said. "What's that?"

My voice sounded ghostlike in the heavy, dripping air.

"I don't know," Henry said, looking in the direction I was pointing.

I pushed hard against the pole and moved the boat toward the tree. Once we were up next to it, I steadied myself as I held on to the trunk. The piece of paper was tacked up with a nail and hung wet and droopy from the rain.

"It looks like some kinda notice," I said, pulling it off the tree and being careful not to rip it.

"Maybe ya shouldn't take it down, Elsie," Henry said, sounding worried.

I ignored his warning and read the words at the top of the paper out loud:

"The Okefenokee Swamp National Wildlife Refuge.

This area now protected by the Agricultural Department of the United States of America."

Underneath the bold print at the top, there was the word *ordinances* and a bunch of numbers followed by a lot of really big words I'd never seen before.

"What does *that* mean?" Henry asked.

"I'm not sure," I said, sitting down and trying to make sense of it.

"Wait a minute!" I said, looking up at Henry. "I bet this is how the president's plannin' on protectin' the Okefenokee. The government's gonna be puttin' a bunch of these signs up to make sure nobody can do anythin' to mess with the swamp."

"They should put yer picture on those notices, Elsie," Henry said happily. "Cuz yer really the one who saved the swamp."

I smiled at Henry. We'd probably never really know for sure if my letter had anything to do with this, but it was nice of him to act like it was all because of me. I still wished I would've had the chance to let Harper know I'd written the letter, because if I really *was* the reason the president decided to save the Okefenokee Swamp and folks found out about it, that would sure be something.

"Ya know what, Henry?" I asked.

"What?" he replied.

"Next time I'm countin' my blessings, I'm gonna count *you*," I said, showing my appreciation for him wanting to give me credit.

Henry James smiled.

"Ya know what else?" I said.

"What?"

"I think we better head back 'fore we both end up pickled from all this rain."

Henry laughed, and I turned the boat around and headed for Honey Island.

Chapter 35

A few days later, Henry and I sat in the front of Uncle Owen's boat on the way to the frolic at Hamp's place on Minnies Island. Huck and Dog sat right next to both of us, and Uncle Owen stood in the back maneuvering his boat through the water as smoothly as Grandma stirred her mixing spoon through cornbread batter.

Grandpa and Grandma were in Grandpa's boat right behind us. And even though Grandma was still real upset about Uncle Lone, Grandpa had talked her into coming to the frolic. He had used a bit of flattery by saying there wouldn't be a reason to frolic at all without Grandma's biscuits and her huckleberry pie.

She had agreed, saying, "Well, I guess our misfortune with Lone shouldn't be a reason fer folks not to have decent biscuits and pie."

As soon as we got close enough to Minnies Island, we heard fiddle and banjo music drifting over the water and through the trees. I couldn't wait to get there so Grandpa's harmonica could join the chorus.

Once we got close enough to see the landing, I heard Farley yell, "They're here!"

And when we got even closer, I saw a big, huge banner stretched between two cypress trees at the swamp's edge.

OUR HOGS ARE HAPPY!
Thanks to Elsie, Henry, and Huck!

Henry and I looked at each other and smiled, and I knew at that moment we had to be the happiest, proudest kids in the entire history of the Okefenokee Swamp.

All the folks at the frolic stood on the landing smiling, waiting to welcome us, and even though I knew Henry James was right about pride being a sin, I had a feeling that God might just be smiling right now too. I even saw Harper there, holding up the *Charlton County Caller*. I felt my face turn redder than Grandma's had that day Harper had devoured her cornbread. Maybe being a hero *was* going to be all I had imagined it to be. In fact, maybe it was going to be even better!

Once our boat reached the landing, folks crowded around us, and Harper held out the newspaper for Henry and me to see. There we were, along with Huck, on the front page.

As everyone moved up the clearing into Hamp's yard, we moved with them. I could barely feel my feet touching the ground. All the attention actually made me glad Grandma had coaxed me into sprucing up a bit and wearing the dress Mama had made me bring along. Soon Grandma and Grandpa joined us in the middle of the crowd, and it was the first time I'd seen Grandma smile since Uncle Lone had gone off to jail.

"I'd like to welcome y'all to this summer's frolic!" Hamp said, standing on his porch steps as everyone gathered around.

The small crowd cheered and whistled and clapped. I had been to the summer frolic every year since I was six, but I had a feeling this year's frolic would be the very best one yet.

"Before we git to the festivities, I think it'd be a good idea to take a few minutes to show our thanks to the Creator of this here swamp," Hamp said.

"Amen!" several folks shouted.

"And this year," Hamp continued, "we have a special young fella who we'd like to have say our blessin'." He paused a minute and looked around at the crowd of folks gathered until his eyes fell on Henry James.

"Henry James, son," Hamp said. "I'd like ya to come on up here and say grace fer us."

"Hallelujah!" Henry James said.

And then he wove his way through the crowd toward Hamp.

Once Henry climbed the porch steps, he cleared his throat and began. "Dear God, we want to thank ya fer our bountiful blessings…"

As Henry went on with his prayer, I couldn't help but think about how he really *would* make a fine preacher someday. In fact, I couldn't imagine Henry James being anything else *but* a preacher.

Once Henry finished his prayer, I heard Harper, who stood next to me, say to Uncle Owen, "I don't know that I've ever heard a better prayer from a preacher."

"Well, that's what Henry's aimin' to do when he grows up," Uncle Owen said, sounding kind of proud of Henry. "He's followin' in his daddy's footsteps."

"Is that right?" Harper said.

"Yeah," Uncle Owen continued. "His daddy and mama are out on a travelin' tent-revival tour right now."

"You don't say," Harper said.

"Yep," Uncle Owen said. "They'll be gone all summer."

"That revival tour wouldn't happen to be in Florida, would it?"

"How'd ya know?" Uncle Owen answered.

"I've got somethin' to show you," Harper said, and he and Uncle Owen headed off toward one of the tables set up in the yard where Harper's cloth bag lay.

I watched them until Henry grabbed me by the arm, pulling me toward the folks at the far end of the yard getting ready for a square dance. The rest of the afternoon passed in a blissful blur because it was all food and fun, music and dancing. From Aunt Eva's fried chicken and mashed potatoes to Aunt Millie's red beans and gravy, I stuffed myself silly. And with Hamp's fiddle and Hatcher's banjo, we never ran out of songs to dance to. Finally, I sat down on a log at the edge of the yard to take a break. Huck loped over and lay down at my feet.

As I sat catching my breath, I saw Hamp trying to teach Henry James how to play his fiddle. I listened to Grandpa play a slow, quiet song on his harmonica as he sat on the porch steps. And I watched Grandma demonstrating to Aunt Millie just how she kneaded the dough for her famous biscuits.

"Being a big hero tiring you out?"

I looked up to see Harper coming toward me.

"No, sir," I said, smiling at him. "Jus' wantin' to savor the moment."

And I was. I wanted to remember this day forever, and I was pretty sure I would.

"You swamp folks really know how to have a good time," Harper said, sitting down next to me.

I smiled at Harper again. Swamp folks *did* know how to have a good time. Actually, they knew more than that. They knew how to have a good life. That's why I loved it here so much.

I reached into my pocket and took out the notice Henry James and I had found posted on that tree. I unfolded the worn and tattered piece of paper. Wanting to keep it with me, when I'd taken off my overalls to get ready for the frolic, I'd stuffed it into the pocket of my dress.

"Guess we've all got a lot be thankful fer with the hogs bein' safe now. 'Sides that, it's nice to know that the Okefenokee is safe now too," I said, looking at the paper in my hands.

It was pure gladness, knowing that none of us had to worry anymore about anything happening to the swamp.

"Where did you get that?" Harper asked, looking at the notice.

"Henry and I found it a few days ago, sir," I answered. "Posted on a tree. We saw a few more of 'em in different places 'round the swamp. I guess from now on folks'll know they can't mess with the Okefenokee."

Harper frowned, but I wasn't sure why.

"Can I take a look at that a minute?" he asked.

I handed it to him, and as Harper studied what was written on the paper, I felt my stomach tighten the way it had when Sheriff Jones told us about Huck. Harper's frown grew worse. He got up and walked over to where Grandpa sat on the porch steps. That tight feeling in my stomach hardened into a rock, and my body felt too heavy to get up and follow him.

I watched Harper sit down next to Grandpa on the steps. He showed Grandpa the paper.

I was too far away to hear what they were saying, but as I watched Harper's serious look, I saw Grandpa's expression turn into disbelief as Harper talked. I was glad I couldn't hear what either of them was saying.

"Hamp!" Grandpa called as he and Harper stood up on the porch steps.

Hamp looked up from the log where he and Henry were sitting for their fiddle lesson.

"C'mere!" Grandpa said.

And as Hamp walked over to Grandpa, I knew that something was terribly wrong.

As Grandpa and Harper talked with Hamp, more and more folks at the frolic—who were scattered around the yard like chickens, enjoying the food, fun, and fellowship—stopped what they were doing to gather around the porch so they could hear what Harper was explaining to Grandpa and Hamp.

Somehow, I pulled myself up from that log where I was sitting and found myself standing on the edge of the crowd, just close enough to listen.

"Well, what does it mean?" I heard Hatcher ask.

"It means, that the government wants to protect and preserve the land so other folks can come visit and enjoy it. But once it's official, since it'll be a wildlife refuge, you folks aren't going to be able to hunt and fish the way you always have," Harper explained. "There will be regulations."

"Regulations?" someone said.

"Yes," Harper continued. "There'll be a quota of how many fish you'll be able to catch and how much wildlife you'll be able to kill. And certain animals will be off limits completely."

"Off limits?" Farley exclaimed.

"Yes," Harper said. "Most likely you won't be able to shoot animals like bears and wildcats."

"But what if they're eating our hogs or chickens or somethin'?" someone asked.

"It won't matter *why* you want to kill them," Harper

explained. "You just won't be able to because the government wants to protect them since there aren't many of them left."

"Protect them," Hamp said. "What 'bout protectin' us?"

"Don't sound like the swamp's saved at all," said Aunt Millie, who was standing right next to Harper. "Sounds more like we lost it fer good."

Silent tears slipped down my cheeks, but before those tears even had a chance to drip off my chin, someone came up behind the crowd standing around Hamp's porch and said, "Pierce County K-9 Unit!"

We all turned around to see a tall, skinny officer standing next to a short, bald-headed one.

My silent tears exploded into sobs, and I fell to the ground and draped myself over Huck, who sat at my feet. I was crying so hard Huck must've thought it was raining.

"One of our officers happened to see an article in the *Charlton County Caller* 'bout a dog y'all been callin' Huck," said the tall, skinny officer.

My sobs turned to heaving gasps of despair.

"Oh, Lord, we need ya now!" Henry wailed from somewhere in the crowd.

When no one else said anything, the short, bald-headed officer said, "So I'm sure ya know why we've come."

"Don't mean we're gonna let ya do what ya come fer."

I looked up to see Grandpa stepping forward from the crowd and toward the officers.

"Sheriff Jones said we could keep the dog," Uncle Owen said, stepping up next to Grandpa.

"Sheriff Jones ain't got no jurisdiction when it comes to property of the Pierce County Sheriff's Department," the skinny officer said, putting his hands on his hips.

"And we've got the papers to prove it," the other officer said, reaching into his pocket, taking out some papers, and unfolding them.

I squeezed my eyes shut, hoping when I opened them again, I'd be up in Grandma and Grandpa's loft to find that this horrible day that had started out as a dream but was ending in a nightmare wasn't really happening at all.

"What if I don't let ya take 'im?" Grandpa asked, putting *his* hands on *his* hips.

"Well, then you'd be under arrest, sir," the first officer said, and the crowd gasped.

Harper stepped forward, took the papers from the officer, studied them, and then handed them back.

"You've got to let them take the dog, Zeke," Harper said sadly. "It's the law."

"Don't know how there can be any law that would take a dog away from a girl who loves him like Elsie Mae loves Huck," Henry spoke up.

"That don't sound like no law to me," Hamp said. "Jus' sounds like human cruelty."

I could barely breathe through my sobs as I felt Grandma's hands on my shoulders pulling me up and off Huck. Then I watched the skinny officer put a leash on Huck. And when he did, Huck pulled against it, but the officer pulled right back, making Huck follow him across the yard, straight toward the landing where the officers' boat waited. I knew if Huck could make any noise, he'd have been whimpering and crying the whole way, but it didn't matter. I was crying enough for both of us.

I thought about the first time I'd laid eyes on Huck. I had thought he looked so pitiful with his droopy ears and extra skin hanging down, but it wasn't any match for how sad I felt now watching him walk away.

It felt like I was sinking in sadness the way people sometimes sank into the swampy ground of the Okefenokee. And just when I was sure the sadness would swallow me up, I felt Henry James standing next to me, whispering the words of Psalm 23 right in my ear.

Chapter 36

The ride home from the frolic was silent except for the sounds of Uncle Owen and Grandpa's paddles and poles digging into the water and my sobbing that had been going on for so long my chest and head ached more than I knew they could. Back at Honey Island, I somehow made it up to the loft and collapsed into bed.

As I lay there staring at the ceiling, I could hear Grandma, Grandpa, Uncle Owen, and Henry down below. It was barely suppertime, but I could hear Grandma fixing food to put on the table, even though I knew no one could be hungry. We had all eaten plenty at the frolic, and even if we hadn't, I didn't see how anyone would have any kind of appetite even for Grandma's cooking.

The rocking chairs by the fireplace creaked, and though

I couldn't see them, I knew Grandpa and Uncle Owen sat in them, pushing the floor of the cabin to make the chairs go back and forth. Henry was probably helping Grandma with the food. No one was talking.

I felt like I was dreaming even though I knew I was wide awake. I had finally stopped crying, but now I lay as limp as tree moss, exhausted from losing all those tears.

I heard the chairs and benches scrape as everyone below me sat down to eat, and I pictured them all bowing their heads and folding their hands.

"Dear Lord, ya know our hearts are heavy t'night, but even so, you've still given us blessin's to be thankful fer…"

Henry's prayer went on and on. Usually, when I sat at the table, I couldn't wait for him to say *amen*, so we could hurry up and eat, but tonight Henry's words sounded comforting.

Once he finally did say *amen*, there wasn't any usual table conversation. How could there be? Today we had all lost the Okefenokee, and I had lost Huck.

I heard bowls being passed and food being scooped, and I imagined they were all taking bites of Grandma's good food, but I also imagined that none of the food could possibly taste anything like it usually did.

"There's no point in waitin' any longer," I heard

Grandpa finally say. "We might as well tell 'im about it now. None of us is eatin' much anyway."

What was going on? Tell who about what?

"Henry James," Grandpa began, sounding serious. "We've got somethin' to tell ya."

I couldn't imagine what Grandpa was going to say.

"Seems yer folks won't be headin' this way fer a good while," Grandpa began.

Oh no! Did something happen to Henry's mama and daddy?

"What?" Henry said, sounding heartbroken. "Why? What happened?"

Even though his words were asking Grandpa to explain, his voice sounded a lot more like he wasn't sure he really wanted to know the answer to his questions.

And though I wasn't even close to being finished feeling sad about Huck, I felt Henry's anxious, worried voice making a lump in my throat the size of Huck's scar.

"Well," Grandpa said, taking a deep breath. "Earlier t'day Uncle Owen and I was talkin' to Harper when we was over at the frolic. He tol' us that all kinds of newspapers from different parts of Georgia and Florida show up at the *Charlton County Caller* newspaper office, and he reads some of 'em now and again. Guess last week he read an article 'bout a travelin' preacher named Harry and his wife, Rhodie."

"Really?" Henry asked, his sadness somehow turning to excitement, even though there was no way what Grandpa had to say could possibly be good news. "What'd it say? I bet Daddy's leadin' so many lost souls to the Lord that they wanted everybody to know 'bout 'im."

"Well, no, not quite," Grandpa said. "Seems that at those tent meetin's, yer mama and daddy've been listenin' to the call of the collection plate instead of listenin' to the call of God."

"What does *that* mean?" Henry asked.

And because I felt like I was watching my life instead of living it, I felt like I was walking in a dream when I got out of bed and crawled over to the edge of the loft so that I could peek down to see everyone sitting around the table.

"It means they stole the missionary offerin' in every single town they visited," Grandpa explained. "And every county sheriff from here to Miami is lookin' fer 'em."

I saw Grandma bite her lip and heard Uncle Owen mumble something under his breath.

"That can't be true," Henry said. "Daddy's out there savin' people's souls."

"Well, it sounds like he's been doin' a li'l more than

that," Grandpa said. "And apparently, yer mama and daddy is now runnin' from the law."

With that, Henry pushed his bench back, jumped up, and ran out the screen door, letting it slap against the house.

"Poor Henry," Grandma said. "With all the good that boy tries t'do, he sure don't deserve none of this."

"The thing is," Uncle Owen said, "Harry's and Rhodie's names won't be cleared from somethin' like this 'less they turn themselves in."

"Well, I can't see 'im doin' that," Grandpa said. "'Specially not after how long Harry spent in Folkston last time he was in there."

"I'd like to git my hands on that sister of mine and knock her from here to Cowhouse Island," Grandma said, her voice sounding a lot like Mama's had the day I dropped her triple-layer coconut cake on the way to the church bake sale. "Rhodie never should've gotten herself tied up with that scraper. I knew he was gonna be nothin' but trouble when she married 'im. He was actin' all born again and holier than thou, and she jus' ate it all up."

Before I even knew what I was doing, I found myself climbing down from the loft and standing in front of Grandpa, Grandma, and Uncle Owen.

"I better go talk to Henry," I heard myself say.

"Want me to go with ya?" Uncle Owen asked.

"No," I said. "I think it'll be better if jus' I go."

And I headed out the door and stood on the porch, looking around the yard for Henry even though I didn't expect to see him. Then I walked down the porch steps, but before going any farther, I looked back at the empty spot beneath the porch swing where Huck used to lay and wished he was there waiting for me to slap my leg and say, "C'mon."

I brushed at another tear that had slipped down my cheek, took a deep, deep breath to keep down the rest of the Huck tears I still had in me, and headed toward the landing to look for Henry.

Chapter 37

Down at the landing, I wasn't surprised to see Uncle Owen's boat gone. I stepped into Grandpa's boat that still rested in the brush at the swamp's edge, grabbed the pole, and shoved off. My chest tightened as I felt the boat slide out into the waterway.

This was the first time all summer I'd been out in the boat without Huck, and it was the first time since Henry and I began searching for those hog bandits that he wasn't with me either.

As I looked around at all the trees tangled together with one another and saw the smooth tea-colored water lapping up against the boat as it cut through the surface, I felt the humid, swampy air pressing my sadness down upon me, and I wondered how I'd ever be able to live without Huck and the Okefenokee Swamp.

And then something pressed down on me so hard I thought it might choke me, and that something was that *I* was the one who brought on all this sadness. It was all on accounta me wanting so desperately to be a hero. I wished like anything I could go back to the beginning of the summer and do everything differently.

But I somehow had to put my own sorrow aside, at least for a while, because Henry James was out in the swamp alone, sinking in his own sadness, and soon it would be dark. Funny how not all that long ago, I wouldn't have cared one little bit about Henry and his preaching parents, but now my heart was just about breaking in two thinking about how awful he must feel.

I pushed hard on the pole, making the boat go faster. I already had a pretty good idea where Henry was, so I pushed the boat along until I was right up next to the narrow channel leading to Hollow Log Pond. I turned the boat between the trees and pushed myself deep into the dark waterway.

If I knew Henry like I thought I did—and I was pretty sure I really did know him after spending every single day with him for practically the whole summer—he'd think that if he went back to Hollow Log Pond by himself, he'd be so scared it might help him forget how sad he was. He also knew getting himself really scared would be the best way to make himself pray, and if anything would cheer Henry's soul at all, talking to the Lord would surely do the trick.

I made my way into the damp darkness that led to Hollow Log Pond, and when I got close, I called out to him, "Heeeeenry! Heeeeenry Jaaaaames!"

I waited and listened for him to answer.

Then I called again, "Heeeenry! Are ya here?"

I was almost all the way to the pond, and I was sure if Henry was there, he could certainly hear me by now. My eyes struggled to adjust to the darkness around me as I searched for him.

Because I had been there so many times with Huck and Henry, Hollow Log Pond felt so familiar now that, for me, it wasn't the least bit scary anymore. But now that Henry wasn't answering me, I felt fear creeping through the tangle of trees, and it was beginning to turn to dread. What if Henry James wasn't here?

"Henry, if you're here, you better answer me!" I called out, my fear sounding like anger.

Not having Henry answer was much scarier than being shot at or being worried that the hog bandits lay hiding somewhere waiting for me.

"I'm right here," I finally heard Henry say.

Now that I'd heard his voice and looked in the direction where it had come from, I saw Uncle Owen's boat wedged between two rows of trees at the far end of the pond. Henry sat on the middle seat with his elbows resting on his knees and his chin resting in his hands. No wonder I hadn't seen him in the darkness until he answered me. It was hard to see him now when I was looking right at him.

"Henry James!" I said, sounding completely exasperated with him. "Why didn't ya answer me? Ya like to scared me to death!"

He didn't even look up, but instead kept staring at the bottom of the boat.

All I could think when I saw Henry was that with as much fussing as Mama did with me about doing my chores and coming home on time for supper and with all the scolding Daddy did about my table manners and getting my schoolwork done, I knew if they ever just up and left me, I'd be about as lost as a gator without water. Besides that, how downright disappointing would it be to have a mama and daddy who stole money from God and then ran from the law?

Now that I was here… Now that I had found Henry… I didn't know what to say.

"I decided somethin' t'night, Elsie," Henry said, filling up the quiet, cool darkness with a voice that didn't sound at all like the one he'd been using to practice his preaching all summer long.

"What?" I asked, moving Grandpa's boat closer so I was just on the other side of the long row of trees right in front of Henry. I looked past the tall, skinny trunks growing up out of the water to stare at Henry, hoping to get him to look at me.

"I'm not gonna be a preacher no more," he said, looking up at me.

I could see why he felt that way. All this time he'd been imitating his daddy, and now he knew his daddy was a big, fat phony.

But the thing was, even though his daddy was a phony, Henry wasn't one. He was sincere. His words were always from the heart. And I could tell he really believed what he said when he preached his sermons. No one should give up on what's in their heart, no matter what.

"Awww, Henry," I said.

"I'm no good at it anyway, and now I know why. It's because my daddy's no good either," Henry said. "He's no good at bein' a preacher. He's not even good at bein' a man."

What could I say to that? Henry's hopes for his life

265

were dashed, and his mama and daddy didn't even care enough about him to turn themselves in so they could come back for him.

I couldn't believe that just a few hours ago, the two of us had been the biggest heroes in all of Charlton County, but now I felt like both of us had great, big burdens we'd be carrying around with us for the rest of our lives.

Chapter 38

The next morning at breakfast, when Henry James prayed, he didn't sound cheerful or earnest the way he usually did. Instead he sounded doubtful and sad.

"We know ya love us and want us to trust ya," Henry began.

I sighed. In front of Grandma, Grandpa, and Uncle Owen, Henry tried to be brave, but I knew that besides what he told me last night about not wanting to be a preacher anymore, Henry's own faith *had* to be wavering.

No one spoke or ate much, and everyone seemed glad when breakfast was over. Grandpa and Uncle Owen headed outside and around the house to work on repairing a hole in the roof of the corn shed, and Grandma busied herself in the kitchen. None of them seemed to know what to do with

Henry and me, so the two of us headed out to the porch and sat on the swing.

The porch felt lonely without Huck, and Uncle Owen had made a point to leave Dog back at his place. Likely he thought seeing Dog hanging around would only be a reminder—not just for me, but for all of us—that Huck was gone.

Henry and I sat for a long time, pushing our toes against the wooden floor of the porch to make the swing creak back and forth through the thick, humid air. We let the creaking sound fill the silent space between us. The pounding of Grandpa and Uncle Owen fixing the corn shed, and Grandma's banging of the breakfast dishes, filled the background with familiar sounds.

"I used to think the Okefenokee Swamp was the Promised Land," I finally said as Henry and I continued to creak and swing. "But now that I've lost Huck and the swamp's gonna be full of restrictions soon, I know how Moses must've felt when he got kicked right out of Canaan."

Henry pressed his feet into the porch floor, stopping the swing.

"Moses didn't git kicked outta the Promised Land, Elsie," Henry said turning to me. "He jus' never got to go *into* the Promised Land. It was punishment fer hittin' that rock, dontcha know that story?"

Of course, I knew that story, but didn't Henry know that I was just making a point? And didn't he know the last thing I needed right now was a Sunday school lesson?

I still felt sorry for Henry on accounta his preacher parents turning criminal, but now that he wasn't out wandering around the swamp and I knew he was safe, I wasn't focused on *his* sorrows as much anymore because mine were crushing my very soul.

I didn't say anything but pushed both my feet hard into the porch floor, jerking the swing back into motion, glad to hear that comforting creak again. Henry's feet joined my rhythm.

"Moses got to *see* the Promised Land," Henry said wistfully to himself, probably because he could tell I was in no mood to listen, "but he jus' never got to go *into* the Promised Land."

Boy, for someone who had decided to give up on his preacher dreams, Henry was still acting a lot like a preacher.

"Well, you know what, Henry?" I said a little too loud, stomping both feet on the floor to stop the swing again.

I turned to look right at Henry. "Then I'm *exactly* like

Moses, because I've *seen* the Promised Land of the Okefenokee Swamp, but I'm never gonna git to live here now. And I've got my own self to thank fer that because of that *dumb* letter I wrote. I also got to see how great it was to have my own dog, but now I don't git to have that anymore either, and it's all my own fault."

I turned away from Henry and jammed my feet against the floor to force the swing back into motion, feeling my sadness turning into mean, hard anger.

"You don't know that yer letter's the reason we're losin' the swamp," Henry James said. "And how could ya know that gitting our picture in the paper would mean you'd lose Huck?"

"Ya said it yerself, Henry. Pride goes before the fall," I said without even looking at him.

"It's not yer fault, Elsie Mae," he said. "Ya never meant fer any of this to happen."

Why did Henry have to be so nice all the time? Even when I was being mean, he was encouraging. Even when he had sorrows of his own, he was kind.

Henry sure didn't deserve my anger. If anyone deserved it, it was me. I just kept thinking if I hadn't been so set on being such a great, big hero, none of this would've happened. I wondered if Uncle Lone felt the same way, sitting over there at Traders Hill waiting for his sentencing.

"Well, I sure don't know why the president had to go make the swamp a refuge, savin' it so a bunch a people who don't even live here could *see* the Okefenokee Swamp, instead of jus' savin' it fer the swampers who actually call it home," I said, trying to turn my anger toward someone other than Henry James.

"Hey, wait a minute," I said, interrupting myself and jumping forward to stop the swing with a jerk. "That might be it!"

"What might be it?" Henry asked.

"Maybe if Grandma, Grandpa, and Uncle Owen could somehow be the ones to *show* people the Okefenokee Swamp, they might still be able to keep livin' in the swamp after all."

"Elsie Mae, yer talkin' jibber-jabber," Henry said.

"Jus' go 'round back and git Grandpa and Uncle Owen and bring 'em 'round to the porch, and I'll go git Grandma," I said. "I might've jus' thought of a way to save a li'l bit of the Promised Land fer all of us."

~ ❈ ~

"So then when Uncle Owen picks up folks from Williamsburg at the Pocket, they pay 'im to give 'em a ride out here to Honey Island," I said excitedly. "Then once they git here, Grandpa

271

gives 'em a tour 'round yer place and shows 'em the hogs and chickens 'round back, lets 'em grind some corn in the corn shed, and maybe even teaches 'em how to make a little syrup too."

Grandpa and Grandma sat in the rocking chairs on the porch staring at me like I was addled, but Uncle Owen, who sat over on the swing with Henry James, looked like the wheels inside his head were turning.

So I went on. "Then, when the tour's all finished up, Grandpa can bring the folks up here to the porch, and Grandma can let 'em have a taste of her best cookin'. Well, let 'em have a taste fer a price, that is. I know folks'd pay a lot of money fer yer biscuits and gravy, and they'd pay even more fer a big slice of huckleberry pie."

"Elsie Mae," Uncle Owen said, "I think ya jus' might have somethin' there."

"But doin' all that ain't gonna change the laws 'bout huntin' and fishin' in the swamp," Grandpa said, not sounding all that convinced.

"Yeah, but, Pa, Harper didn't say we wouldn't be able to hunt and fish at all," Uncle Owen said. "He jus' said there'd be limits, and we won't need to hunt and fish near as much if we was makin' money from the folks comin' to visit us in the swamp."

"I suppose yer right 'bout that," Grandpa said.

"It would be fun to have folks come and enjoy my cookin'," Grandma said. "Do ya really think folks'd pay fer it?"

"*That* I know fer a fact!" Grandpa said, smiling.

"And the best part is you'd git to stay livin' right here on Honey Island," I said.

"Hallelujah, Elsie Mae!" Henry said.

Chapter 39

About a week later, Uncle Owen and Henry James took his boat and Grandpa's boat over to the Pocket to pick up our first group of visitors.

Just after I had told everyone my idea for the Honey Island Okefenokee Promised Land Swamp Tours, Uncle Owen, Henry James, and I had made a couple signs advertising our tours and brought them over to Williamsburg, the town just west of the Pocket, and today was the day of our very first tour.

Even though getting everything ready for this big day couldn't ever fill up the empty hole in my heart where Huck used to live, it was at least helping to ease my heartache just a bit.

I still wasn't sure my letter had really had anything to

do with the president's plan for turning the Okefenokee into a wildlife refuge. But in case my letter did have something to do with it, I was at least glad my plan for the Honey Island Okefenokee Promised Land Swamp Tours might make it possible for Grandma and Grandpa to keep living on Honey Island.

While Uncle Owen and Henry James were gone picking up the folks we hoped were waiting at the Pocket for our first-ever tour, Grandpa was out back making sure that there was plenty of feed for folks to give the chickens and plenty of corn in the corn shed for folks to try their hand at grinding it. And out on the porch, I helped Grandma arrange her pie slices and her jars of tea.

"Elsie Mae," Grandma said, "this was a darn good idea ya had, but I'm awful nervous 'bout strangers tastin' my pie."

"Why should ya be nervous 'bout that?" I said. "Any folks I know who taste yer pie say it's the best in the whole swamp."

"But maybe folks outside the swamp won't think so," Grandma said, sounding worried. "And I don't want to be takin' money from no one if they don't like my pie."

"Grandma," I said. "Stop worryin'. Folks aren't jus' gonna *like* yer pie, they're gonna love it!"

"I hope so," Grandma said. "Why don't ya be a good girl and run 'round back and check on yer grandpa?"

But before I had a chance to answer we heard, "*Yeeeeowwwweeee! Yeeeowwwweee!*" It was Uncle Owen, letting us know he was close.

"I'm goin' down to the landing to wait fer 'em and see how many folks are here," I said, hurrying down the porch steps.

When I got to the swamp's edge to welcome our first visitors, I was surprised to see Harper and the two officers from the Pierce County K-9 Department standing side by side on the landing. My stomach tightened. What were *they* doing here?

"There she is!" Harper said. "The only person I know with just enough spunk to write a letter to the president himself."

What was Harper talking about?

"Well, I'd say that calls fer some kinda reward," the tall, skinny officer said.

"Only reward good 'nough fer spunk like that is this!" the bald-headed officer said as he stepped aside.

And there was Huck sitting in the officers' boat.

Tears spilled down my cheeks one after the other at the sight of my dog.

Were they really giving Huck back to me as a reward? I was too afraid to even hope.

But before I could find my voice to ask any questions, Huck loped out of the boat and was right there at my feet where he always used to be, and I collapsed in a heap on top of him, burying my face in his neck.

"What's goin' on?" I heard Uncle Owen ask as his boat slid up on the landing next to the officers' boat.

"We're jus' here deliverin' a li'l reward to a girl who deserves one," the tall, skinny officer said.

I looked up to see confusion on Uncle Owen's face, and the family he had picked up at the Pocket looked even more confused and a little worried too. Likely they wondered why a couple of K-9 officers had shown up on their Promised Land Swamp Tour.

"I was doing a little digging for a story I was working on, and I found out something very interesting," Harper began. "I don't know if you know this or not, Owen, but your niece wrote a letter to the president of the United States and sent it all the way to the White House. Well, come to find out, that letter of hers ended up playing a pretty big part in getting the president to declare the Okefenokee Swamp a National Wildlife Refuge."

"Ya mean Elsie Mae saved the swamp from that ship canal?" Uncle Owen asked.

"That's exactly what I mean," Harper answered.

"But I lost the swamp fer folks who call it home," I

said, feeling the responsibility of what I had done pressing against my happiness about Huck and giving my stomach an awful feeling.

"Yeah, but we're figurin' it out," Uncle Owen said, looking at the people in his boat who had come for the tour.

"And, Elsie Mae," Harper added, "because of you, the Okefenokee will be preserved forever for generations to come."

"And that ain't no small thing," the bald-headed officer added.

"Hallelujah!" Henry James said as he slid Grandpa's boat up onto the landing right next to Uncle Owen's.

He had a couple more folks with him that had come for the swamp tour.

"When Harper come up to Pierce County to tell us about Elsie's Mae's letter," the tall, skinny officer went on to explain, "we all agreed that gittin' Huck back was the only reward good 'nough fer somethin' like what she done."

I couldn't believe it! It was a better reward than getting a million dollars. I squeezed Huck so tight, I thought I might just suffocate him.

"Let's go tell Grandma and Grandpa the good news!" I said. "C'mon, Huck!"

It felt so good to slap my leg and race up the trail toward

the house with Huck following behind me, and I laughed and cried to myself the whole time I ran.

"Grandma! Grandpa!" I shouted.

They were both waiting for me in the yard by the time I came running through the gate, and when they saw Huck, Grandma said, "Elsie Mae!" and then she started to cry.

And when Grandpa didn't say anything, but cleared his throat more than a few times, I had a feeling he was doing everything he could not to cry.

Once Henry James, Uncle Owen, the swamp tour visitors, the K-9 officers, and Harper got up to the yard, Uncle Owen introduced everyone, and Harper filled Grandma and Grandpa in on the reason why Huck was mine again.

And after more tears, and even more laughter, and a few hallelujahs from Henry James, Grandpa and Henry brought the swamp visitors around back so they could feed the chickens, pet the hogs, and grind some corn. Then they brought them around to the porch to join Uncle Owen, Harper, and the two officers, who were already devouring Grandma's pie and guzzling down her tea so fast I thought she'd have to make more. And every single person on the swamp tour bought a slice of pie and a jar of tea, and then all of us sat together on the porch as if we were part of the same big, happy family.

But I knew I was the happiest member of that family because Huck was sitting at my feet, right where he always belonged.

Besides that, it looked like my idea for the swamp tours had a chance of really working. Giving folks a glimpse of life here in the Okefenokee might mean we'd get to keep holding on to a piece of our Promised Land at least for the time being.

Maybe being a hero had made a lot of good things happen after all.

Even so, later when our first swamp tour visitors were getting ready to leave Honey Island, Harper pulled me aside to say, "So, Elsie, I'd like to hear how you got the idea for the swamp tours. I'd love to write about it in the *Charlton County Caller*. Maybe even drum up some business for you kind folks."

But I didn't take any glory for it.

I told him it was all Henry James's idea, and that Henry was the one who deserved all the credit. After all, it was Henry's preaching ways that caused me to even be thinking about the Promised Land. Besides that, now that I had experienced being a hero, as good as it felt, it didn't seem all that important to be one anymore.

Chapter 40

After our first Honey Island Promised Land Swamp Tour, summer was winding down. I would be going home to Waycross soon, and Henry was going to be leaving Honey Island too.

After a few late nights talking with Grandma and Grandpa, Uncle Owen had decided that with Henry's parents on the run and Uncle Lone in Folkston Prison, Henry James should come live with him. That meant Uncle Owen would have to move to Williamsburg so that Henry James could go to school. Uncle Owen thought that would be better in the long run since it was closer to the Pocket, where he planned to pick up folks every weekend for the Promised Land Swamp Tours.

Henry and I knew we only had a few days of Okefenokee freedom left.

We wanted to make the most of the short time we had, so we were out in Uncle Owen's boat with Huck and Dog. We headed through the waterway leading toward Billys Lake. We planned to go back to Hollow Log Pond once more just for old time's sake.

"Ya know, Henry," I said as we got closer to the dark channel leading to the pond. "Ya can't jus' give up on yer dream of becomin' a travelin' preacher cuz of yer daddy."

"It's not really got nothin' t'do with my daddy," Henry said. "I can't be a preacher cuz I'm no good."

"Who says yer no good?" I asked, lookin' over my shoulder as I pushed hard on the pole, moving our boat along.

"Well…" Henry said, stalling a little.

"Ya don't mean cuz of the stuff Uncle Lone used to say about ya, do ya?" I asked, turning back around. "Look at where his orneriness landed him… right in Folkston Prison."

As I said those words out loud, I felt that familiar twinge of guilt. Maybe I had been hanging around Henry James too long if I was feeling guilty about stuff even when he wasn't quoting scripture and trying to make me feel that way.

When I thought about Uncle Lone now after all that had happened this summer, I kind of felt sorry for him. Maybe he wasn't as ornery on the inside as he looked to be on the outside. Maybe he just acted that way because he wanted people to pay attention to him for doing something good, but things just never turned out the way he wanted them to. I sure knew how that felt.

"No, it's not cuz of Uncle Lone," Henry said.

"Then what?"

Henry was quiet, and all I could hear were the tiny splashes I made every time I dug the pole into the water to push at the swampy ground.

"Henry, jus' tell me."

I turned around, leaning on the pole and putting one hand on my hip.

"You," Henry James said. "You're the reason."

"*Me!*"

What was Henry talking about? Maybe at the beginning of the summer I'd done some things to make him feel like I didn't think he'd make a good preacher, but a lot had changed since then. We had captured the hog bandits together and saved the swamp, not just from the ship company, but together we had found a way for Grandma and Grandpa to keep living here, helping them save their way of life at least for a while. Even more than all that, we were friends now, best friends.

"Henry James Mason, I *never* said you were no good at preachin'!" I exclaimed, dropping the pole to the bottom of the boat so I could put *both* hands on my hips.

"Ya didn't have to *say* it," Henry said, getting louder. "Elsie Mae, I preached to ya all summer long! I practiced my best sermons on ya! I quoted scripture like I was John the Baptist himself! I prayed fer yer very soul, and even baptized ya, and nothin' happened!"

I took my hands off my hips and sat down in the boat and rested my elbows on my knees and looked at Henry.

"And that's not jus' cuz my mama and daddy are crooks," Henry said. "Mus' be I ain't got the Spirit in me if I did all that, and ya ain't changed one little bit."

I wondered how someone with such a good heart could've ended up with a couple of phonies for parents. Henry deserved so much better.

Henry rested his chin in his hands and looked down.

The thing is I *had* changed. When Henry had first gotten to the swamp this summer, I couldn't stand him *or* his hallelujahs, but now we were the best of friends, just as Grandpa had predicted. And at the start of the summer, if someone would've told me that I would end up being happy about sharing the glory of saving the swamp with Henry, I would've said that was crazier than a coon playing a fiddle. But now I couldn't imagine having saved the swamp without him. In fact, I couldn't imagine having had *any* fun this summer without Henry.

"Henry," I said. "I have a confession to make."

"It's too late now to pretend like ya want to confess yer sins and be born again," Henry mumbled.

"No, not that kind of confession," I said. "Remember when we were out in Billys Lake fer my baptism?"

"Yeah."

"Well, I think I might a felt somethin'," I said.

"Yer jus' sayin' that to make me feel better," he said.

"No, really," I said. "I felt somethin' inside, and I don't think it was jus' me being scared of the gators. I think it might could've been the Spirit."

Henry picked up his head to look at me.

"Why didn't ya say anythin' 'bout it before?" he asked, sounding suspicious.

"I don't know," I said. "I guess I didn't know if it was anythin' real, but then when ya said a minute ago that I didn't change, I thought 'bout all that's happened this summer, and the truth is I *have* changed, and I think it's all because of *you*, Henry."

"Really?" Henry said, sounding like his old preacher self again.

"Really."

"Well, ya mean cuz of me and the Spirit," Henry said.

Good old humble Henry.

"Yeah. You and the Spirit."

"Well, *HALLELUJAH!*" Henry shouted, his voice echoing off the water and making his hallelujah sound louder than Uncle Owen's loudest swamp call. "The Lord does work in mysterious ways, doesn't he, Elsie Mae?"

"Yeah, I'll say. He ended up makin' the two of us friends, didn't he?" I said, grinning at Henry.

"That's not mysterious," Henry James said, smiling. "That's a downright miracle from above."

And we both laughed.

I stood up and finished pushing the boat all the way into Hollow Log Pond, and when we got there, I sat down, looked around in the darkness, and listened to the quiet. Everyone else thought this pond was good for nothing, but because of all that had happened here, it would always be special to me.

Henry James stood up in the boat, "Let's praise the heavenly Father," he said, closing his eyes and lifting his hands way up high as if he could reach past the cypress branches and all the way up to heaven.

And as he prayed one of his absolute most flowery and scripture-filled prayers (that I knew was going to go on way too long) I thought about how thankful I was that Henry James had barged right into my summer. I knew I would never hold up my hands and pray like *he* did, but even so there might be more than a few times I'd whisper how grateful I was for a friend like Henry James, who not only made my summer turn out better than I ever though it could, but also somehow made me a better me, which turned out to be even more satisfying than being a hero.

A Note from the Author

Naturalist Francis Harper began studying the Okefenokee Swamp in the early 1900s. In his numerous trips to the swamp, with the intent of studying the flora and fauna, a surprising thing happened. Francis fell in love with the people of the Okefenokee—the swampers. These Georgia pioneers, or Crackers as they were sometimes called, lived on the islands of the Okefenokee, sustaining generation after generation, by living off the rich and plentiful land of the swamp.

Because of Francis's affection and admiration for these swampers, his documentation on swamp life began to include more and more about the people who lived there. He had such a heart for this unusual and mysterious place and the exceptionally resourceful and warm and welcoming people who lived in it, that over the years, Francis not only *studied* the swamp but he also lived there with his family on different occasions for extended periods of time. The swamp in a way became a second home for the Harpers.

Over the years in which he studied the swamp, Francis saw many changes in the Okefenokee. By the mid-1930s, the swampers' way of life began to be influenced by the outside world as inventions such as the radio provided a means of connecting to life outside the Okefenokee. Francis realized that the simple swamper life he had grown to love would soon disappear as young people attended nearby public schools and chose to move away from the swamp in search of new opportunities.

But for Harper, some of the most disheartening changes were the influences which endangered the very existence of the swamp, such as a lumber company stripping the land of its valuable cypress trees or a ship company with plans to build a canal through the waterways of the Okefenokee. These things which threatened the preservation of the swamp caused Francis's wife, Jean, to use her connection to President Roosevelt (she had been a tutor for his children at one time) to write to the president asking for his help in preserving the Okefenokee. Her husband's work, her letters, and the efforts made by some of the great-great grandchildren of the original swampers were instrumental in President Roosevelt's Executive Order that the Okefenokee Swamp become a National Wildlife Refuge preserving it for generations to come.

Though the National Wildlife Refuge status, given to the Okefenokee in 1937, certainly preserved the beauty and mystery of the Okefenokee, it also inadvertently brought on the demise of the swamper way of life. With new laws and regulations about hunting and fishing in the Okefenokee, the swampers could no longer provide for their families and live off the land the way they had done for so many generations in the past. The swamper families still living in the Okefenokee were forced to move to nearby towns. The swamp was saved, but the swamper way of life was lost forever—only the memories of those who had experienced it would remain.

Though the specific events and characters in *Elsie Mae Has Something to Say* are fiction, the slice of history described above provided the inspiration for Elsie Mae's story. It is with great appreciation for all those who had a part in ensuring the preservation of the Okefenokee and for all those who cared enough to record the history of the swampers who lived there, that I have come to write this book.

It is my hope that Elsie Mae's story captures the heart and soul of the mysterious place called the Okefenokee Swamp.

An Additional Note Regarding the Time Frame of Events in Elsie Mae Has Something to Say

In 1933, Francis Harper's wife, Jean, wrote her first letter to President Roosevelt making him aware of the ship canal project that threatened the beauty and wildlife of the Okefenokee Swamp. Though Roosevelt did respond to her letter, it wasn't until 1935, after Jean Harper had written him another letter, that he informed her of his support to make the preservation of the Okefenokee a special project. The president's support led to an Executive Order establishing the Okefenokee Swamp as a Wildlife Refuge in March 1937.

Elsie Mae's story begins with her letter to the president in May 1933 and ends with the Okefenokee Swamp being declared a Wildlife Refuge just a few short months later. My reason for condensing what happened historically is three-fold. First, for a novel this length, it was necessary for me to keep events to a reasonable amount of time. Second, I wanted readers to have the opportunity to see Okefenokee Swamp life in a more simple and untouched state. With every year that passed, the influences of the outside world impacted the culture of the swamper families who called the Okefenokee home, chipping away at the uniqueness of swamp culture. Setting the story in 1933 allowed me to let readers see more of the swampers' one-of-a-kind way of life. Third, having the story take place in 1933 makes the story more plausible in terms of other historic and natural events that happened in and around that time such as lumber companies setting up shop in the swamp and swamp fires that ravaged but then rejuvenated the growth of the Okefenokee Swamp.

Glossary

A few Okefenokee words you may not know:

Addled: mentally weak or crazy

Frolic: social gathering with square dancing to guitar, banjo, and fiddle music

Scraper: a quarrelsome person or a person up to no good

Shim-shacking: loafing or wasting time

Bibliography

Harper, Francis and Delma E. Presley. *Okefinokee Album*. Athens, Georgia: The University of Georgia Press, 1981.

Mays, Lois Barefoot and Richard H. Mays. *Queen of the Okefenokee*. Folkston, Georgia: Okefenokee Press, 2003.

Mays, Lois Barefoot. *Settlers of the Okefenokee: Seven Biographical Sketches*. Jacksonville, Florida: Rascoe Photo/Type, 1975.

McQueen, A. S. and Hamp Mizell. *History of Okefenokee Swamp*. Tallahassee, Florida: Rose Printing Company, Inc., 1926.

Nelson, Megan Kate. *Trembling Earth: A Cultural History of the Okefenokee Swamp*. Athens, Georgia: University of Georgia Press, 2005.

Velie, Eugene. *Billy's Island Okefenokee's Mystery Island*. Waycross, Georgia: Brantley Printing Company, 1992.

Acknowledgments

First, thank you to Francis Harper and his family for their work and unending affection for the Okefenokee Swamp and the swampers who lived there. His book *Okefinokee Album* is the seed from which this story grew. A special thank-you to his wife, Jean, who cared enough to write a letter. What an amazing example of the power of words!

Second, a huge thank-you to Dorinda L. Montgomery for putting me in touch with Lois Mays and Ron A. Phernetton. Lois and Ron, I can't begin to tell you how grateful I am for the hours you spent helping me get the details of this story right. Your wealth of information is invaluable, and your willingness to share it is remarkable! I felt the kindness of those early swampers in your patient enthusiasm.

And thank you to Diane Nelson and Patty Toht for

taking time to read my finished manuscript. Your encouragement came at a time when I needed confidence to know my story was not just clear in my own mind, but would also be clear in the mind of my readers.

A shout-out to my first critique group, who oh so many, many years ago listened to this story in a variety of versions. Greg Daigle, Patty Toht, Ruth VanderZee, Ellen Carroll, Darcy Zoells, and Michelle Schaub, thank you for your wonderful feedback and patient encouragement.

And what do I say about the wonderful folks at Sourcebooks? The only thing I can say is that, because of all of you and what you do, I feel like the luckiest author in the world. Dominique Raccah, *your* dreams keep making more of *my* dreams come true, so thank you for that! And Steve Geck, thank you for being the kind of editor who says things like, "You've written a novel that's easy to love." Words like that allow an author to soar!

Which leads me to my next thank-you to Holly Root, who has continued to be the steady hand that keeps my writing career on course. Working with you is so much my pleasure!

And Mom and Dad, thank you for always being supportive and encouraging. You are perfect "author parents" because you aren't afraid to be bold with bookmarks and bookstores. And thank you Susan and Scott, you both make perfect "author siblings" since you don't mind bragging about your sister to anyone who may or may not be interested in listening to you talk about my books.

As always, a special thanks to Ron and Chaylee for listening to me go on and on with my latest swamper story, for putting up with the heat, bugs, snakes, and gators when we visited the Okefenokee on vacation, and for letting me spend so many hours in my office with my imagination and these characters, creating their story. You are both the best!

Finally, a huge "Hallelujah!" for all the blessings that keep coming down from above which are always more than I can ask or imagine. My cup overflows!

About the Author

Nancy J. Cavanaugh is the acclaimed author of *Always, Abigail*, a Texas Bluebonnet Award nominee, and *This Journal Belongs to Ratchet*, a Florida State Library Book Award winner, an NCTE Notable Children's Book in the Language Arts Award winner, and nominee for numerous state awards, including Florida Sunshine State Young Reader's Award and Illinois Rebecca Caudill Young Readers' Book Award. She's a former teacher and library media specialist. She and her husband and daughter enjoy winters in sunny Florida and eat pizza in Chicago the rest of the year.